MEDITERRANEAN STORIES—

Innocent & Profane

Sandy McCulloch

To Carol —

In friendship

Sandy

PREMIERE EDITIONS INTERNATIONAL, INC.
CORVALLIS, OREGON

PREMIERE EDITIONS INTERNATIONAL, INC.
2397 NW Kings Blvd. #311
Corvallis, Oregon 97330
TELEPHONE: (541) 752-4239 – FAX (541) 752-4463
INTERNET: *www.premiere-editions.com*

GRAPHICS EDITOR
— René L. Redelsperger

AUTHOR PORTRAIT PHOTOGRAPHER
— Stephen Meyer

PRINTED IN THE UNITED STATES OF AMERICA
CASCADE PRINTING COMPANY, CORVALLIS, OREGON

ISBN: 1-891519-02-6
Library of Congress Catalog Card Number:
99-66298

for
Linda Lancione Moyer
without whom ...

"*A*ll living souls welcome what they are able to cope with. All else they ignore, or pronounce to be monstrous and wrong, or deny to be possible."

—SANTAYANA

ACKNOWLEDGMENTS

Many individuals helped in the shaping of this book, but a handful of people made particularly important contributions:

Linda Lancione Moyer, Gerry Huckaby,
Mary Ann Airth, Suzin Shumway,
Moira Dempsey, Aysegul Manav,
and especially Dr. Mary Johnson,
Dr. Kay Dieter and Irene Gresick

STORY CONTENTS

MEDITERRANEAN PLACES —

BULGARIA

Istanbul

Ankara

TURKEY

Antalya

SYRIA

ALBANIA

GREECE

Beirut

Athens

Kas Simena

LEBANON

CRETE

*Cyclades

ISRAEL

Alexandria

Matruh

EGYPT

LIBYA

*The Cyclades of
Greece include:
    Amorgos
    Naxos
    Milos
    Kato Andikeri
    Koufonissi
    Keros

INTRODUCTION

This is a book of stories about the ordinary people of the Mediterranean ports. I have tried to write about them as they really are—people quite different from my own country and from Europe north of the Alps. It is sometimes difficult to write about the people and things that one loves; therefore, it is only fair to speak of my origins and my cultural bias. I first traveled to Greece in 1983 and in perhaps a week I had fallen in love with the country. Only some years later, after my first travels in Italy and Turkey, did I realize that I had fallen in love not simply with one country or its people, but rather with the people of the entire Mediterranean. My own cultural roots are largely Germanic; and on a sunlit October day some years ago a German schoolteacher on Santorini said to me, "I came here to enjoy the sun for a week, because I looked at the sky and realized that soon I was not going to see the sun for six months."

"I have loved the Mediterranean with passion, no doubt because I am a northerner." These are the first words of Fernand Braudel's monumental and encyclopedic *The Mediterranean.* And it serves quite well as a summary of the past seventeen years of my own life, except that I am not terribly concerned with the sun or the mountains or the sea. My interests lie almost entirely in the people. I have loved greatly the people of the Mediterranean, their connectedness, their warmth and generosity and kindness, their basic humanity and—at least in contrast

to my own world—their closeness to God. And I have done my best to write of them as they really are. I believe, with Braudel, that the Mediterranean is a single world—and that its people share a common culture. The ordinary people of the ports, from Tangier to Istanbul and from Marseille to Alexandria, have much in common.

Each of us lives within the stream of our own culture and our own personal realities, but occasionally we all go traveling. If we cannot go traveling in our ordinary reality, on a plane or a train, then we travel in our imagination. When we read stories about the travel of others in foreign lands, surely it is partly in the hope that this "travel literature" will allow us to experience a small taste of these other worlds. In one of the most marvelous passages in 20th century literature, Paul Bowles described some of the unorthodox religious practices of the desert Berbers of Morocco. They did not observe the fast of Ramadan properly, and did not veil or segregate their women. And during gigantic pilgramages,

"...men and women together dance themselves into a prolonged frenzy which can last for thirty-six hours at a stretch. Self-torture, the inducing of trances, ordeal by fire and sword, and eating of such delicacies as broken glass and scorpions are also usual..."

"To me these spectacles are filled with great beauty, because their obvious purpose is to prove the superiority of the spirit over the flesh. The sight of ten or twenty thousand people actively declaring their faith, demonstrating en masse the power of that faith, can scarcely be anything but inspiring. You lie in the

fire, I gash my legs and arms with a knife, he pounds a sharpened bone into his thigh with a rock–then, together, covered with ashes and blood, we sing and dance in joyous praise of the saint and the god who make it possible for us to triumph over pain and, by extension, over death itself."

What is marvelous to me about these lines is that Bowles takes us to a different world—paints a picture in words—does not morally judge what he sees—and then in his imagination invites participation. He paints a word-picture, and a participation: *"you lie in the fire, I gash my legs and arms...we sing and dance....."* You. I. We.

It is a convention, both among travelers and among many who serve them, to divide the visitors into "tourists" or "travelers." The latter, of course, travel more slowly and at least in small ways make contact with ordinary people. However, Pico Iyer recently suggested a more meaningful distinction—between those who leave their assumptions at home, and those who do not. Iyer, who may be the most thoughtful travel writer in late 20th century English literature, was interviewed in the *Los Angeles Times* in April, 1998. He put it this way:

"...for me, the first great joy of traveling is simply the luxury of leaving all my beliefs and certainties at home and seeing everything I thought I knew in a different light–"

Iyer quotes the Harvard philosopher George Santayana as saying,

"We need sometimes...to escape into open solitudes, into timeliness, into the moral holiday of running some pure hazard, in order to sharpen the edge of life, to taste hardship, and to be compelled to work desperately for a moment at no matter what."

I happen to be extremely fond of Santayana's idea of the *"moral holiday."* How can we imagine the inner realities of another person without taking a moral holiday? Some of the characters in my stories are simple honest country-people, ethical shopkeepers, or ordinary people of almost incomprehensible warmth, generosity and kindness. A few might even be saints. On the other hand, some are thieves, prostitutes, forgers, smugglers, and dealers in stolen goods and black money. The problem is, these people also love their children, just as you and I.

Most of these stories are descriptive non-fiction, some of them are fiction, and some are a mixture of both. I cannot always tell the difference. The stories are usually narrated in the first-person singular; this has been a convention in oratory and literature for millennia—it is simply the strongest form. But in all of these stories, whatever the form, I have tried to be faithful to one idea: I have tried to write of people just as they are. Perhaps the supreme virtue in storytelling is to try to be simple. I have tried to write simply. And I have attempted in these stories to take a moral holiday—to write about people simply as they are. Each of us has all of humanity within us—and we hide it so well.

THE PIANO ON KATO ANDIKERI

One day as I stood on the quay at Katapola, Amorgos, a big white fishing boat came out of the west. It had no trim of bright color, and was running with a gaff-rigged sail pulled so high to the mast that in the distance it might have been a lanteen. It carried no fishing gear, but otherwise it was an ordinary Greek caique, a fish-boat. It was called the EVDOKIA, and from it came a powerfully built, poised man whose name, I later learned, was Vangilis. Staring at the caique, I said to a Greek standing nearby, "Where did that boat come from?" And he replied, "Kato Andikeri." Frustrated, thinking this a harbor I'd never heard of, somewhere in the Cyclades, I ask impatiently, "What island?" And with growing impatience, the response was *Kato Andikeri, Kato Andikeri.* I had visited all of the 24 occupied Cyclades, and had never heard of such a place. Eventually I learned that perhaps ten miles directly west from the long, protected harbor of Katapola sat two tiny islands known as Ano and Kato Andikeri. A pair, separated by only a very narrow channel, they lay just south of the large, uninhabited, once-sacred island of Keros; their names translate as Upper and Lower Next-to-Keros. These people were telling me the EVDOKIA came from this tiny island, surely less than a mile across, called Lower Next-to-Keros. What an unlikely idea. But it was true.

For many years the tiny pair had belonged to a family of Amorgos, and forty years ago several people had lived there and herded a few goats and sheep. Gradually, over the years, the young people grew up and went to Athens; this is the story of the islands in the late 20th Century. I was told that only Vangilis lived there now, in a little white house near the top of Kato Andikeri, and that a few years ago he had sold Ano Andikeri to a Greek investor. Now, the Andikeris are merely tiny, low hilltops poking out of the wind-battered sea. They carry little vegetation, for the Greek still herds a few of the goats that maintain the normal barren, deforested state of most Cycladic islands. In winter such small islands are ghastly places for human inhabitants, much less a solitary man. The gulls scream, a boat may not come or go for ten or twenty days at a time, and even a saint might be sorely tried. To me, Vangilis seemed a very solid man, but—a saint? I learned that he spent much of his time in Katapola, and probably came and went on whim. The Greek was not a full-time resident of his tiny lump of rock.

I was told that a second little white stone house sits low on Kato Andikeri, just over the channel that separates the pair of islets. This is said to be the occasional home of an old and very odd one-armed French doctor who sometimes comes in the summer. The French is said to appear "like a ghost," with odd eyes and a wispy beard. None of that seemed strange to me, all French are odd. But then I was told two last bits of extraordinary information. Each of the little rock houses on Kato Andikeri had one unusual possession: on this tiny islet, with no electricity, no roads, no store, no nothing, the Greek had a telephone (Koufonissi exchange) and the Frenchman had a piano!

Everything I have told you, up to this point, apparently is a fact; it is all supported by evidence, or the word of more than one man. Now, a fact is a very nice thing, it can be picked up, and turned over, and examined. A fact has a certain weight, if you will. However, the rest of this story cannot be verified. It is told only by one old woman of dubious reputation. But I think it may be true. Even if it is all lies, still it may be true.

She was a young nomad German girl with a slack bony body and slack, questionable morals; the sort who hitch-hikes everywhere, pays for nothing, and in our age probably would wear a ring in her nose. Be that as it may, the German girl had two rare talents: she spoke almost perfect French—and she had certain abilities with the piano. Traveling in the Cyclades, she heard about the one-armed French with the piano. The girl hitched a ride on a Greek fishing boat—God knows how she managed that—and had the caique drop her on the shore of Kato Andikeri. The fisherman offered to wait. "The French is crazy, he won't let you stay. I will wait until you talk to him."

"But no! He can't make me swim off into the sea! I want you gone!" So the fisherman left.

The Frenchman was appalled at the bony little German at his doorstep. "You can't stay! Go away!" said the French.

"But I can't go," said Frauke (her name sounded something like that.) "I can't leave, my caique is gone! But," she said in perfect French, "if you will play the piano for me, and answer one question, then I will go sleep on the shore and never come near your house again. If that is what you want."

The French walked to his piano and played the left hand notes from a Bach prelude with his left arm and hand. "The question, quickly," he said to the German.

"I was told," said the girl, "that you lost your right arm after the piano came here, only a few years ago. How can you play, so well, only the notes for the left hand?"

"Because I can hear the other notes in my head perfectly, I can hear them, I CAN HEAR THEM. GET OUT OF MY HOUSE."

He rushed at the young Frauke and pushed her to the door. She scampered around him at the last second and ran to the piano. "DO THEY SOUND LIKE THIS?" she shouted, and her right hand fell on the keyboard, and out of the piano poured only the notes for the right hand. The French stood listening, frozen into marble, for perhaps ten seconds. Then he began to cry. Then he sat at the piano, still crying, and began to play the left hand. The two played together, side by side, and played very well, for a long time. The only thing the girl ever volunteered was, "Thank God you chose Bach. I couldn't have done Debussy." Finally the French asked how she, the girl, could play only the one hand. "I can also hear the other hand," she said. "A few people can...."

"You can stay here as long as you like," said the French, "if you will play the right hand."

"Done," she said, and she made a small bad joke. "I shall be your right hand man." And for a long time she lived with the Frenchman. He played the left hand, she played the right hand, and they never had much else to do with each other except at the piano. She slept outside most of the time, in the warm nights under the fire of the stars. Sometimes, when he allowed it, she would cook for him. Sometimes, about once a month, one of them would go to Katapola with the Greek to buy supplies. The Greek would give them fish. Once in awhile the Greek or the Frenchman would slaughter a kid. But only rarely did they talk. The piano was their conversation and their communion, their sacrament, their flesh and blood of Christ.

The Frenchman never lied to Frauke—unless silence is a lie, and his silence did not feel like a lie. But once, Frauke lied to him. After she had stayed four or five months, she said to him, "I should go to Athens to get my other clothes and my tools."

At this, the French asked her, "Your tools for what kind of work?" And she lied....

The girl took a ride to Katapola with the Greek, hitched a ride on a boat to Athens, and in a few days returned to Kato Andikeri with a small bag of things. Now all of her few things were there. "I missed the music," said the French—and for him this was a huge admission. So they played Bach and some Beethoven sonatas all through one long night, while a full moon fell upon the island and the gulls, besotted with the moonlight and the music, flew about until exhausted. Perhaps neither the Frenchman nor the girl were happy people. For that matter, neither, perhaps, was the Greek, Vangilis. None of us can know, really, what is in the mind of another. The three were all outsiders. But the three surely were content. For a while the three lived their uneventful lives, with the goats and the music and the sea, and no tears fell on Kato Andikeri. And in country Greece a day is counted as happy if it passes without tears.

Then came a day when the French said to the girl, "I go with Vangilis to Katapola for the dentist. Back tomorrow, probably. Play both hands, you must not forget how." This was as close as the French came to humor, he was a cautious man.

The Frauke seemed bored, said, "see you," or some such, and idled by the door while the Greek raised his sail and the EVDOKIA ran down-wind into the East. She waited carefully by the door, looking out over the beautiful sea, until the sail disappeared in the distance. Then, safely alone on Kato Andikeri, she ran for her bag. She went to the piano with the few tools of her trade. She laid her tools neatly on a chair beside the piano bench. And then she tuned the piano.

Kato Andikeri had never seen a road, crime, electricity, a doctor or a policeman, and it had certainly never seen a piano-tuner. The piano had not been tuned in years. It was a perfectly good baby-grand, but now— well, after years out of tune in the salt air it would never again, for long, hold its tune. The Frauke did her best, which was quite good. She was very happy, which is not the same as contented. The Frauke was happy, proud of herself, even joyful, as she thought about how much pleasure this surprise gift would give her French friend. And, truly, now the piano had beautiful sound. It also sounded... different.

That night the Frelke did not sleep well. She played both hands on the piano, relishing its new beauty. On the following day she sat in the doorway, impatient in her anticipation, and happy with her cleverness, until the EVDOKIA came out of the East under engine. Soon the Frenchman came to the door, tired and with his face stiff from the dentist. Speechless, the girl ran to the piano and played the opening of a Bach sonata ... and a violent blow on the side of her head hurled her to the floor. The Frenchman stood over her screaming,

"What did you do to the piano? What did you do to the piano?"

Shocked and stunned, her face torn and bleeding, she stared up at him from the floor and said, "*I tuned the piano. I am a piano-tuner. I don't understand—what is wrong? What is wrong?*" In agony the Frenchman shouted down at her, "*It's different!*" "*The piano's changed, you broke it! It's different!*"

"No," she said pathetically, "I just tuned it."

But the French screamed at her, "*It's different. I can't hear the music anymore.* I CAN'T HEAR THE MUSIC." And then the Frenchman took out of his pocket the heavy knife that was used to cut the throat of the goats. His eyes, always gray and dim, now were as lifeless as the furrowed skin of his face.   Looking up from the stone floor, Frauke saw the last light leaving his eyes and she understood.

ONE LEGO MISSING

Kas is a town of perhaps five thousand on the Mediterranean coast of Turkey. Thirty years ago Kas probably had little cash economy, and many who knew this beautiful village even fifteen years ago say it is now ruined by a busy summer tourist industry. But Kas is lovely. The entire region is littered with pre-Christian relics. In the center of town, one block back from the port, a narrow pedestrian street climbs gently two blocks up a hill to a 2500 year old Lycian pedestal tomb. The lane is decorated with masses of bougainvillaea and other flowering vines, and many tiny porches from the Ottoman period hang beautifully over the street. The lane is charming, and could even be accused of being quaint. It is the home of perhaps twenty-five or thirty small shops dealing with the tourist trade, and the best of these are the two shops of Martina and Orhan Yilmaz. (Antiques, nautical instruments, prints, carpets.) As I talked with Orhan in his shop one morning, his two-year-old baby girl happily ran into the shop and out again. Repeatedly she ran in and out, and down the street. Orhan ignored her disappearances, and I became curious.

"Is it so safe here that you don't need to see where she has gone?"

Orhan walked to the door, looked up and down the street, and said quite firmly, "Everybody knows everybody else here, no one would let her go past the end of the block in either direction. We all take care of each other." Then Orhan paused, and looked a hundred feet down the lane to where a shop was closed, the front covered with a sheet metal screen. "See the shop that is closed? One Lego is missing."

I was stunned. How could I have imagined that children's toys, the tightly connecting *Lego®* blocks, had joined the universal language of *taxi, okay, bravo,* and *no problem.* But here were Legos® on the south coast of Turkey, as a metaphor for connection. My mind raced to the Greek who had said in 1970, "We are still a primitive enough people so that we are still connected to each other." And a few months later, when 16-year-old Diamado Andricopoulos heard this story, sitting on the curb by her father's shop in the Plaka of Athens, she laughed and said,

"It's the same here. When I was five or six I decided I was going up to the Acropolis by myself." She looked up the street to where the great Acropolis of Athens stood against the sky, and continued, "I got as far as the end of the block. The last shop is owned by another Kostis, same name as my father. He asked, 'Diamado, where are you going?' 'Up there,' I replied, pointing. He asked a couple more questions, then stepped out and roared down the street, 'ANDRICOPOULOS'!! I have never forgiven him for telling my father."

In the small villages of the Greek Cycladic Islands it is the same, the tiny children are simply watched over collectively by the village. In Folegandros Chora I once watched a beautiful, brightly dressed and extremely active two-year-old named Daphne as she explored the three village squares at nightfall. Gradually the people were disappearing, going home to dinner, and Daphne finally seemed to be abandoned, left alone in the dusk. I became casually protective, kept track of her for a few minutes, and then realized that at least one set of eyes was watching, always, from a doorway or a taverna nearby. As she dashed about, apparently alone, the village was watching over her.

Back in Kas, after the Lego remark, several of us were talking about Mediterranean hospitality. I mentioned that on two occasions Americans had told me of being invited to spend a long weekend, or a week, with country Greek families. They arrived, and were introduced to the children, shown the home and the farm, the buildings and the animals, and in each case were shown a room and told, "This is your bedroom, and that is your bed. Make yourself at home." Eventually, in each case, it dawned on the visitor: *This is the only bed in this home.* Where are the Mama and the Papa going to sleep? Where? On mats on the kitchen floor. Furthermore, after a week-long visit one family ran a little short on bread and the visitor could not correct the matter without insult. They all ate what the family could afford.

When I told this story a Canadian woman of perhaps fifty-five responded, "Let me tell you MY story!" A frequent visitor to Kas, she had arrived one spring, gone to the Pension where she had always stayed, and was greeted by a shocked innkeeper who said,

"Judy! You can't come here now! There is absolutely no room available in Kas! It is Bayram, the Sacrifice Festival. Kas is full, I can't help you!"

"Well, I am here. Please, Mustafa, try to find me something. Anything....."

"Yes, I will find something. But it won't be much. I will do my best." And, an hour later, "Yes, I have found a room for you. Since they are poor people, they will accept $10 a night. But they want it understood that you are their honored guest. It is not for the money. You are their guest. They will be happy if you will eat with them." The Canadian went, stayed a week, and had a wonderful time. She felt greatly cared for. The home had two rooms. One bedroom with one bed—hers. And one large combination living room and kitchen—where the family intended to sleep on mats. THE FAMILY WAS TWELVE. The parents were finally persuaded that three children should put their sleeping mats in her room. When Judy reminisced about that visit, these were her words:

"That week I remember as a happy time among friends. I treasure it. I return to Turkey each year because of the people, the warmth, generosity, trust, and friendship from everyone I meet. I've thought for years about staying. *My family in Canada—really is not family. They love me at their convenience.* That's a hard thing to admit, but it is true. Going home to Canada is always difficult. I cry when I leave here—it is so sad to leave a home, a country, where I am completely accepted. We consider Turkey a third world country—but it is more advanced than North America."

This Canadian, and many visitors, are quickly struck by the trust and honesty of the Turkish. Leave a camera on your table in an outdoor café in Naples, and it will be gone before you close the toilet door. However, my traveling companion once left a video-camera at our table in an outdoor café in Bodrum, Turkey. She came to her senses an hour later, raced back to the café in the forlorn hope that it would still be there, and was greeted by the smiling manager holding the camera. "Do not worry," he said, "if you had come back next year, it would still have been waiting for you!"

On hearing this story, another traveler in the gathering in Kas remarked that seventy years ago in Spain a person, on leaving home, might put the key in the outside lock of the door. This was to tell any visitor, *We're not home, but if you need anything, or want to visit, just come in.* An American bystander, who had lived in Kas for seven years, immediately said, *My landlady and landlord do that now, today. If they are away, the key on the outside means, "We're out - but come in and make yourself at home. Welcome!"*

On countless occasions in both Greece and Turkey, in large cities and in small villages, I have been offered free lodging, or have had strangers go blocks out of their way to guide me to some obscure place. The generosity takes many forms. In Istanbul one summer, after I had bought my *International Herald Tribune* at the same news stand early each morning for a week, I arrived one day around noon. The seller looked at me with unhappy surprise, and instantly said, "We are out! I thought you had already come!" "No problem," said I, and started to leave. "No, wait," he said, and then he was on the phone; and then he said firmly,

"I have called a bookstore and newspaper stand three blocks from here. They still have a copy of the *Tribune* and they are saving it for you. Go there now. And after this I will be sure always to save a copy for you."

Perhaps all of this could be summed up by a remark of Dr. Oguz Onder that I have mentioned elsewhere. When I needed to spend two days in the International Hospital of Istanbul, he gave me excellent care, and exchanged currency for me, and concerned himself with my needs regarding a hotel, and a taxi. After a parting conversation in which I thanked Dr. Onder profusely several times, he finally said in a low voice, *We must take care of each other.*

A few years ago a bomb exploded in a marketplace in Beirut, Lebanon. Moments later a man carrying a bleeding child flagged down a passing taxi and leapt in, crying, "The hospital! The hospital!" As the taxi raced for a hospital carrying the man, the child, and another passenger, he held the blood-covered body in his arms and screamed over and over,
  "Hurry up, my child is bleeding!" Then he was screaming,
  "Hurry up, my child is unconscious!" Soon he was screaming,
  "Hurry up, my child is not breathing!"
And then, as they neared the hospital, finally,
  "Hurry up, my child is cold!"
  When they arrived at the emergency room, the man and the other passenger rushed the child to a doctor. The child was dead. The man forlornly turned to walk away and the doctor said,
  "Wait, I need to know your child's name."
  "I don't know his name." And the taxi passenger instantly said,
  "I thought he was your child!"
  The blood soaked man looked about, and said,
  "Aren't they **all** our children?"

Postscript:

In the 1970's a friend of mine in California, a woman named DiFranza, said she had seen a rather violent movie—that she really liked because it also reminded her of the loving Italian family of her childhood. That movie was rather successful, and a *New Yorker* article [3/24/97] examined its appeal. It spoke of the disintegration of the American family. Here, in this movie, "was this role model of a family who stuck together, who'd die for one another. The real appeal of the movie was showing family ties in a setting of power." It was "a perverse expression of a desirable and lost cultural tradition, filling people with longing for a family like that..." (...a family that would even kill for you.)

The movie was called, *The Godfather.*

THEY DON'T EAT PEOPLE
IN BUENOS AIRES

*I*magine vast numbers of people living on the platforms of a railway station. The platforms are densely crowded, horribly dirty and noisy; in the confusion and disorder, many among the destitute and the crippled are pushed to the edge of the platforms and they and their children are pushed off and killed by oncoming trains. Others board the trains, which have four possible destinations: War, Hunger, Disease, and Ignorance. These people and their children live on the edge of an abyss. They are the vast poor of Egypt. Their children, many of them, are absolute angels. Since they are angels, truly, and since the people have so little else, I dare to say that they love their children more than we do.

Living on the edge of the abyss, in Egypt the poor or discouraged will do almost anything to survive and find a better life for their children. They may offer a child to a foreigner, if he or she will take the child to a better world. Some would sell one to feed the others. A woman may offer her body—or a man will offer it. Beautiful young women would marry a European for a passport. A decently dressed young man stopped me on the street and asked where I was from. On hearing, he instantly pleaded quietly with me to find him an American wife so that he could reach my country. If one wishes to judge, this business runs the gamut from the sad to the evil. However, evil exists. Eldridge

Cleaver wrote of "...the black ghetto where the dark and vicious deeds appear not as aberrations or deviations from the norm, but as part of the sufficiency of the Evil of the day....." And Ghandi remarked that for a man who goes without two meals a day, "the only form in which God dare appear is food..." I would add that if God does not appear, terrible things may happen.

In October of 1997 I met Ahmed at the mid-town bus plaza in Alexandria. He was a man of perhaps fifty, graying and becoming stout, he was dignified and warm and straightforward. At first. After a few minutes he told me about his wife and son and daughter, and said they would all be pleased and honored if I would come to their home for a dinner. It would be a pleasure for them all ... I guessed at the time that they were warm, kind-hearted working-class people and that I might be the first foreign visitor, almost certainly the first American, to come to their table. Ahmed and I agreed to meet at one o'clock the next day at the same place and share a lunch. He was on time, remarkable in this world. However, he announced not a nearby bit to eat, but a visit to his home. His family was delighted I was coming. His wife was preparing a good Egyptian meal. We set off in a taxi. And very soon I was hearing remarkable words, and the alarm bells were ringing loudly in my brain. Ahmed announced that I could stay with them. They would give me their big double bed, the best one, and they would sleep in the other room. I had heard of this kind of hospitality in Greece and Turkey—the honored guest gets the best or only bed, in the best or only bedroom, and the mama and papa and kids sleep on mats on the floors. I had never imagined such an offer

for myself. However, during the taxi ride Ahmed borrowed—no, requested—money to buy needed food and drink. And he also made a series of uncalled for and remarkable statements, such as,
"I am not a pimp."
"I am not a thief."
"I am not a liar."
"We are good people."
Such remarks continued through the entire day, as well as remarks like, "It is very safe to eat these leafy vegetables, my wife washes them with a chemical to kill all the diseases." Thank you.

During the taxi ride Ahmed also asked casually about my sexual preferences. Well, the fact is, I am a physical coward. All my life I have forced myself to do what I wish to do, over-riding my cowardly self. But right then? I stayed in that taxi, and did not leap out into the kind slums of Alexandria, for only one reason; all intuition said that a friendly wife, daughter, and son really did exist and were looking forward to my arrival. And that a good Egyptian meal and warm hospitality did await us. And this was indeed correct. Ahmed's daughter, Nadia, was eight years old, a shy little angel with long trails of black hair in a braid. When prompted, she left the room, undid the braid, and delightedly came back to show me her waist-long little mane. Her brother, Karim, was sixteen, slender, reserved, and had a sparkling smile. Ahmed said he had studied English, had seldom spoken it, but understood a good bit. Ahmed also said he was an outstanding soccer player and attended the main Sports Gymnasium (high school) in Alexandria. (Of this, more later.) These children seemed very loving toward their parents and one another, and were charming toward the strange American.

Ahmed's wife, Mona, was 36, heavy, dark, with black hair, and beautiful. She had a strong, handsome Arab face full of vitality and strength. Her smile was warm and open. Her eyes glittered with amused, seductive, arch, playful lights. In a grade B Mediterranean movie she would knife the man who abused her. In *Rigoletto* she would be cast as the Sicilian mistress of Sparafucile, the assassin. Mona spoke no English with her mouth, but she spoke much with her face. And after a half an hour of warm greetings—the giving of small gifts and announcements regarding dinner to come—she was ordering Ahmed to tell me that Mona *likes me*. She likes me. I have a warm smile, a good heart. In fact, Mona likes this exotic foreigner so much that *Mona would like to share her bed with me—and pretty much intends to do that this afternoon. And would I like to do that?* Her eyes glittered with play and curiosity. I looked down at the floor under my feet, and cracks were spreading in all directions. There were loud crackling sounds and then I fell through the surface of the world. I had believed Isaac Bashevis Singer when he wrote, "*People are the same the world over. They don't eat people in Buenos Aires either.*" Well, Singer was wrong. They do eat people in Alexandria. Mona wanted me for dessert. In the meantime I was now supposed to sit still for a good Egyptian meal—and digest it—while my brain screamed, *this absolutely should not be happening in a Muslim country. It should not.*

We sat for perhaps an hour and a half over an excellent Egyptian dinner. We chatted cordially, with Ahmed translating and Karim understanding it all. Then the children were sent off to the gym. When I think back to that afternoon, the recurring word is *nightmare,* but a nightmare primarily in one specific sense. In the Mediterranean, privacy generally is not highly regarded. The Greek word for a private man is *idios,* idiot; if you sit alone, you must be ill. Arabic, I am told, has no word for privacy in the sense of "I want my privacy, want my private space." When the children were out of sight or out of the flat, *all* was explicit and *nothing* was private. *Nothing.* They talked about *everything.* It was a nightmare. I travel in order to know and enjoy other worlds and other people as they truly are, in all of their manifestations. Now I had found a manifest nightmare; and my brain was shouting, *Why? Why is this happening?*

It seems to me that I had three choices: I could run screaming out of the flat into the dirt streets of southern Alexandria. Or I could bed the woman. And third—if I did that—I could then wait in Alexandria to see if the police, a rape charge and blackmail were Act III of this theater. However, that seemed unlikely. Mona was a warm, lusty open book. The humanity poured out of her eyes like warm honey out of a jug. What was happening was clearly her willing choice, she was not operating from a con—at least not for gain alone—but from lust and curiosity. I would not care to have this woman really angry at me—not that it was a possibility —but would I care to accept the gift of affection? I could have said no. I didn't want to. Mona had me for dessert. I had Mona for dessert. Dessert was indigestible, the man kept wandering into the room. [Were you expecting that sin would result in pleasure, or go unpunished? That is not the way of the world.]

Later Mona announced that she wanted a baby from the nice American. Ahmed announced that he couldn't afford another. But if I would promise to come and visit my child, and send small support, then *Enshallah* - God willing—a baby. *Don't ask. I don't know what I was doing, or why. [Yes, I do.] How can I even write down this insanity. My flesh crawls...*

During the first day, Ahmed indicated in many different ways that he might be a thief, but I did not judge that he would steal from me. He was after larger gain, not petty thievery: He looked for material gain, but WHAT? WHY? Eaten alive by curiosity at the entire business, I stayed in touch with the family for about ten days. I shared another meal with them. And I gave him two hundred dollars to take the entire family and myself for a three-day holiday to the beaches of Marsa Matruh. That weekend did not come off quite as planned because of a death in the family, but it was nevertheless worth every penny and more. I have described part of that trip elsewhere in a story called *At Table With Seaside Bedouins.*

Eventually, many days later, Ahmed's plans for me became clear. I guessed them, and finally he made it clear. This little man would do anything, absolutely anything, to get his children to a better life in the United States. He would give them away—he would give his wife away—if this would get them to his imagined promised land. Perhaps he then expected that he could follow them. These were people, like so many in the Third World, who live on the edge of dire poverty. On the edge of the abyss. The children were as described, they were sweet, warm beings. Absolutely wonderful kids. Ahmed especially was fixed upon the idea that he might get his beautiful son to the U.S. Karim was one of six hundred students at the boys Sports Gymnasium of Alexandria. Ahmed took me to the principal, and to teachers. He also took me to the main football stadium of Alexandria, where I was introduced to coaches and watched Karim in a practice game. Ahmed seemed to know all these people, and preened himself noisily in their company. But the main point—to be driven home to me—was that Karim was a star football player, and should merit an athletic scholarship at a U.S. university.

I am not at all sure Ahmed wanted the U.S. for himself. But clearly he no longer wanted his wife. He wanted short-term gain for himself, and especially he wanted the U.S. for his two kids. He begged small sums of money hourly. He lied. Cheated. In a dozen ways he seemed a rotten human being. But he had lovely children. Repeatedly I asked myself, how could such a rotten man have such a good product? Must be good in him I cannot see ...

As for Mona? This is Constantine Cavafy's *Sensual Alexandria*. This is the city that Lawrence Durrell said had the most beautiful women in the world. In a letter to Henry Miller written from Alexandria during World War II—with bombs falling and the city in fear, life and death hysteria, as Rommel's tank corps crept ever closer —Durrell said that "*... One has never had anything lovelier and emptier than an Alexandrian girl. Their very emptiness is a caress.*"

Early on that first evening Ahmed and I left the apartment, and before he dropped me at my hotel we went shopping at the Nobar Souk. Ahmed was buying a goose—chosen alive and butchered—and many supplies for tomorrow's dinner. [I was supposed to join them, but did not.] At night the huge Souk was a boiling, screaming din. Flatbeds, cars, pickups, taxis, horse-drawn wagons and passenger carriages and man-pulled carts pushed through the mob of men, women and children. Blocks and blocks were jammed with fruit, vegetables, meat, live goats, poultry and rabbits, live birds to eat, fish, nuts, cheese, oil, hardware. Men shouted and threatened, blows were thrown, the air was full of laughter and music and pure noise. The main street blazed with naked light bulbs. The side lanes were black with shadows and poverty. Foodstuffs were piled up in small mountains, raw, often dirty, and filled with nourishment. Poor country women sat on the filthy ground along the edges of the streets with tired piles of wilted vegetables before them in the blackness. The figs were bursting, streaming their sweet juice everywhere. Mango and sugar cane were piled and stacked all about. In the midst of this din, two geese were copulating by the side of the street. Three other geese were loudly objecting. In the sad little flats above the Souk people were copulating, perhaps being born, dying. On the street animals were being slaughtered, in the dark side lanes derelict old people waited for death. All of the life cycle was there: Copulation, birth, growth, struggle, slaughter, death. All of it .....

By the time I left Alexandria, I had concluded that Ahmed was a rather short-sighted and greed-blinded hustler. He lied too much and listened too seldom to be an effective con man. I very much doubted that he would harm me, but two Alex friends said that he would be dangerous when he knew I was departing. They strongly urged me to go without a goodbye, and I did so.

My friendship with Mona—and it *was* a friendship— was a more complicated matter. In the beginning I surely was no more than a satisfactory means to an end, and possibly an entertainment. However, in the end we did share a real affection.

For years I had carried in my day-pack a gold wedding band that I would never wear again. It had little resale value and bad associations for me, and at one time I had nearly thrown it into the sea. At our last meeting, I gave Mona the ring and told Ahmed to translate to her that in my country we have a custom called a "friendship ring." Her response was to examine it [It is real gold?] and place it on a middle finger, where it fit. I told her that if she ever needed to, she could sell it. She stared at me, and Ahmed translated, *"I want to cry. I will never sell it. I will always wear it to remember you by."* I think she knew then—it was in her voice—that she would never see me again.

Postscript:
For many years Alexandria has been one of the great cities of the world and also one of its notorious flesh-pots. From the magnificent and often erotic poetry of the great Greek poet, Constantine Cavafy, to the erotic chaos of Lawrence Durrell's *Alexandria Quartet,* this was one of the great Bad Cities of the world. Since the Nasser revolution of the 1950s, all of that is supposed to have passed away. Nonsense. Recently a Kuwaiti who had done five years of University in Alexandria said to me, *"I loved Alexandria! The women are very good and beautiful and cheap."* [Ugh.]
Underneath the surface scratching of Calvin Klein® and Marlboros® and cellular phones, very old places change only gradually. Men and women pass by and away, but the theater remains. When young we believe that the world is for us, but when old we discover that we are for it. They do eat people in Alexandria. In *A Private Correspondence,* Durrell also said of the Alexandrians that *"when they make love it's like two people in a dark room slashing at each other with razors—."*

YASMINA—THE GIRL WHO RAN

*K*oufonissi is a tiny, flat, dry island in the remote eastern Cycladic Islands. The one town is home to a few hundred fisher-people, friendly and kind and intelligent people leading simple lives. The surrounding sea is beautiful beyond imagining. Yet a few years ago on nearby Amorgos I had heard a rumor of a terrible thing: *the most beautiful girl on Koufonissi had simply disappeared in the middle of the night.*

At the back of the town beach on Koufonissi sits a small hotel and, on the ground floor, a rather dirty little general store and *cafenion.* Here one can sit in the dying light of the evening, watch the children play soccer on the beach, and look across the aquamarine straits to the once-sacred island of Keros. And here one evening an old woman sat down at my table—no Greek woman should do that—and ordered a coffee.

"You come here two weeks ago," she said, "and ask the people about the girl who ran away. You speak some Greek. So I think you should know the people won't talk about this. Who are you? What do you do, sitting here and waiting? Like a Greek who has nothing to do all day." The old woman spoke quite good English, probably she was not from here. I answered her.

"So, you are a writer. You make a lot of money writing about us. No? Then you are a fool. And you think—now I will tell about the girl who ran. No? Well, I don't." She sat and drank her coffee, stared at me, very self-possessed, and then said, "No, I don't tell you about the girl. The people here have enough pain. But I will tell you a different story." This is the story she told.

Once upon a time, almost ninety years ago, a little girl was born on a tiny island not far south from here. One village of a hundred souls. That island, that village, are now abandoned. But then it was very beautiful, a tiny valley came down from the hills, a tiny stream in winter and spring. We would grow vegetables. The valley supported olive, grape, fig, lemons, bees. We had the goats and the fish. We traded for wheat from the bigger islands. Except for wheat and tobacco we had all we needed. When I was a child I thought my island had all that any man could want. That was correct. But I was not a man.

My name then was Maria. The island was called Acanthonissi. These are not important, both names are gone now and you will not find the name of my island on any map. We are all abandoned. But Maria was the most beautiful girl on that island. She was the princess of Acanthonissi, she was beloved. In a village of one hundred, such a child is its very heart, its pride, its celebration. Until I was seventeen.... Until I was seventeen I literally had never asked for anything. Nothing of any weight. All was given to me. But then came a day and an hour I shall remember always.

"Father, I have never been away. Not even to great Naxos, that we see to the North on clear days. Once, before you find me a husband, let me see Naxos, maybe even once go to Athens. Please."

"No. You are too young. Later."

I literally had not imagined they would say No. I, the princess who had never asked for anything. I, who always rose silently and gave my father my chair if he tapped me on my shoulder. I who had not once ever raised my voice to them.

"I AM GROWN," I screamed. **"I AM GROWN."**

"Later."

"I am grown, and I have always obeyed you. I want to visit Naxos."

"LATER."

"I am going to visit Naxos," I said. Then I was beaten.

I never raised my voice to him or asked for anything again. Now I knew what hate meant. Now I knew what I was, and it was not a princess. I left my parents, walked to the beach, walked into the warm and shallow sea up to my knees, and looked into the far distance. I had loved best my family and the magnificent sea. Now I looked at the sea, felt the wet circles around my legs, and I hated my father. The sea felt like poison around my legs. I hated the sea. The sea had become my jailor. Now I knew. I would wait for "later."

A year later, later came. It came in the form of a beautiful 20-meter sailboat, with six English, anchored off the town beach in calm summer weather. The men of my village had told the fishermen from other islands never to bring foreigners here. The one thing they could not prevent was the occasional yacht that would pass by in summer, see the village, and anchor off the town beach out of simple curiosity. Here was such a boat, and the six English came ashore in late afternoon.

My village, although old, was very pretty in the light of the failing sun. The English were fed a good dinner of fresh fish and lobster. I was not allowed near them, of course, and would not have been able to talk to them at any rate. But a prisoner looks for only one bit, one fragment of information that leads to freedom. I saw that among the English was one woman, and saw her treated with respect. With these English I would be safe. Enough.

The English boat stayed at anchor off the town beach for the night, as I thought it would. I waited until the part of the night when sleep is deepest. Wrapped a few clothes into a ball. And I left my people a message they would understand. When a Greek girl goes into a nunnery, she cuts off all her hair. It is an act of utter renunciation. I slipped into the kitchen, stole the sharpest knife, cut off my great mane of black hair, and I left it on the floor of my room. My people would see my hair, and known pain. Then I went to the English, swimming the hundred meters or so to their boat with the clothes held above my head and the knife in my belt. I rested for a moment with one hand on the boat. There was no sound anywhere, on water or land. I lifted my bundle of clothes onto the deck, put one leg on the low gunwale, and rolled gently over onto the deck. As I did the knife slipped from my belt and dropped a few inches onto the deck with a small noise.

If a man is standing watch on a boat at night in calm weather, he may doze off. There is no likely danger; and the man sleeps lightly, awakens easily. A few moments after I boarded the boat, a crewman sleepily came on deck. He was the watch, he had heard the knife drop, and he stared at me with such shock that for a moment I saw myself as he did. I had never been self-conscious. I had taken off my outer clothes to swim out to the boat. I was an apparition! In the middle of the night a half-naked girl with no hair had risen out of the sea and now stood on his deck! He stared at my hand. I looked down. I was a half-naked girl with no hair *and a large knife in my hand!* I had forgotten, I had picked it up after it fell. I jammed the knife back in my belt. Fiercely, waiving my arms—without any words, we had none in common—I made him understand:

I am going with you. Now. You do not want to be here in the morning. They—I waved my fists toward the silent village—they will be very angry.

I went to the bow, gesturing for him to follow, and began taking in the one bow anchor. He hesitated. I stupidly waved my knife at him for emphasis, but he understood. We took in the anchor. I was much stronger than he. In the silence of the night, in a very light breeze, we raised one large foresail—what the English call a Genoa. The beautiful wooden boat began to turn ever so slowly toward the south; slowly, as slowly as a ballet in slow motion, it turned. The Genoa began to fill, the boat began to ghost away. I looked up, ahead of us to the south; and saw the most wonderful sight I have ever seen. Low in the night sky hung a yellow full moon. Below it on the flat sea was a glittering gold sea-road, a band of yellow-gold so bright it seemed solid. The sailboat had pirouetted, turned down this glittering sea-road, slowly gathered way, and on this road we slid away into the bright south. I have never been back to my island.

We sat in silence for many moments. I was stunned. It was a little too dramatic—but this was a Greek, and it was, after all, her story. Who was I to argue? I wanted more.... Finally she spoke.

"I won't tell you much more, there are fifty stories like that. I am old and tired, and after all it is not your business. I only tell you because you snoop about the girl who ran away from here. Now do you understand why we leave?"

"No. No, I don't. If you had demanded to visit Naxos, eventually they would have yielded. You were a princess."

"I see. You don't understand Greece. Listen. A Greek girl like me, on a small island, is almost always cast out. Look. The English were very kind to me. Many days later I left them at Paros, but I have always loved the English. Always in the Cyclades there has been a community of ex-patriots from their Empire. Maugham—yes, stupid one, I am an old Greek woman in black rags, but I have read the English, I lived in London. Maugham wrote beautifully about these ex-patriots when the Empire still existed. Exiles all have the burden of meaningless lives, the burden of hating their own. And so, they sit in the café with their ouzo—with no purpose in their lives—and slowly lose their control, and then their teeth and then they die. It is a terrible thing to reject one's own."

"I found the English colony on Paros, and left the English boat. But after the English departed, it took me only a week to be outcast on *this* island. No Greek girl can sit alone in the café, but I do what I want. One evening the Greek fishermen at the port café began what they called "arm wrestling." I watched, saw how it was done, not only with the shoulder but also the brain. I asked to try. The fishermen laughed at me. That was a serious mistake, to my way of thinking. Uninvited, I sat down opposite the biggest—but not the strongest—fisherman in the café. I took his hand, I looked at him in the eye and said, in a little girl voice, *You laugh at me?* He laughed at me again, as he was supposed to, and as he laughed I very nearly broke his wrist over the edge of the table. The man put his arm back in place, but quickly, before he was ready to start I did it again. I found that on strength alone I could beat half the fishermen on Paros. Some of the rest could be tricked. But toward the end of the night, a night of joyful combat and laughter, suddenly I looked around the café and realized what I had done. All the English were roaring with laughter. Not one Greek was laughing. Not one. On Paros, too, I was done for. Now I could be the lover of drunken Englishmen. That was all that was left for me. *Now*, do you understand?"

"*Now, do you understand*? Shit. *Idios! Idios!* Idiot. Look around, look around you on the town beach, this café, on Koufonissi. What do you see? *Tell me.*"

I was bewildered, because I thought I understood, but I spoke: "I see children playing on the town beach, old people walking along the water. A fishing boat unloading. Keros. In the distance, Amorgos. I see a beautiful bay with blue and green water.... What do you *want* me to see?"

"Now, think. Do you see death here, American? Life? Do you know the Greek, *Metaphora*? You do know the term metaphor—"

"I'm sorry, I don't know what you want."

"American, *look around you*. Here in the café, what do you see?" (Now I was in despair.)

"I see tables and chairs. Dirty dishes at one table. A pile of left-over spaghetti, with sauce, and flies. An empty tuna can on the floor. An old boat engine on concrete blocks. An old oil can with an old, dry, half-dead oregano plant. A dead Jasmine in a big pot; in the pot there are many cigarette butts. *What do you want me to say?"* I was almost ready to scream at her.

The old woman smiled, and I saw that she enjoyed my frustration. *"Tell me,* she said, tell me more about the plants. The oregano is like me—old, dry, half dead. But you are wrong about the Jasmine, it is not yet quite gone."

I looked, carefully; and began to suspect where I was being led. This was all about the Jasmine. Then I was sure, and gave her what she wanted. "The Jasmine is in a big pot, but it has not been watered. It has been left to die. Last spring, when it was planted, the young plant had good earth and water. And the vine, as it grew taller, was fastened against the side of the building. But there is a roof over the outside porch of this café, the Jasmine has never had enough light. When a plant needs light, it grows taller and taller—as tall as it can. The side branches die off, the lower leaves die off, all growth is at the tip, the highest point. Desperately the tip seeks for light. In nature, it would try to climb above the others. Every plant must have light. Now it is October. Fastened against the concrete wall, the Jasmine has climbed fourteen feet. The soil is now exhausted, the water is gone, winter is coming. When a flowering plant is dying, its last act will be to flower. [If a plant were thoughtful, it would be saying, Maybe the seeds will survive.] This Jasmine has spent all of its year seeking light. It has climbed fourteen feet. And now it has reached the end, for immediately above it is solid, corrugated sheet metal death. Death. Tucked up just under the sheet metal roof, floating in the near-darkness, are two little puffs of white flowers. And now the Jasmine is going to die."

"I tell you an ironic thing, American. Country Greece is an Arab country. And in the Arab countries many little girls are named Jasmine. Once my name was Maria, but now... now my name is Yasmina. Now... you understand."

VINO DEL CASA

*I*t was yet another Sicilian, years later, who finally allowed Melissa to admit the truth about Salvatore. He had told her of the wonderful sweet wines of Sicily, about the *Zibibo*, and the magnificent *Muscato*. And Luigi had explained the importance of late harvest. If the grape is picked too early it contains little sugar, and makes a very ordinary wine. This is drunk by the ordinary people and the poor, or sold by the barrel and then poured into an open bottle for tourists. "We call it VINO DEL CASA, house wine," said Luigi. "The secret of the good vino is to take the grape as late as possible. One must wait. The later in the fall it is picked, the sweeter the grape, and the sweetest of all we call *Late, Late Harvest*. The grapes are taken so late they are beginning to loose the water, they fall if the vine is touched, they make the superb *Muscato* of Sicily, of Pantellaria. These wines have enormous fragrance and the aftertaste, the lingering flavor, lasts. Lasts for a lifetime. Bella! Bella!" This is Melissa's story essentially as she told it to me.

I was sixteen and very beautiful, a sexy street-wise girl from Berkeley, California. I went to Italy. I went by myself. I was no virgin child, I thought I knew how to take care of myself. I did know. Thinking back, I would even have described myself as a good girl, but in the Mediterranean there are only two kinds of girls: good girls and bad girls. I didn't know that, I didn't know the rules. Which city? No matter, I won't say, it could have happened anywhere; it could have been wicked Palermo or, just as easily, gentle Florence. It was Italy. Italy peeled me like a grape.

For three days I had a simply wonderful Italian summer vacation, an idyll, a dream. On the fourth day, in the early afternoon, at the counter of an ice cream shop, a voice from my left spoke to me in Italian. I remember exactly where I was at that moment. And the voice came from the left, from above. I turned and looked up - into the most beautiful face I have ever seen in my entire life. *How* beautiful? *Devastating.* Olive skin, long black straight hair, a classic Italian face filled with enormous warm and gentle green eyes. The eyes were smiling. They were filled with laughter, they were smiling, and they were *smiling at me.* For just a second or two I froze, and then inside of me everything simply melted down. Inside, I just collapsed. An insane voice was shouting, silently, *Anything you want, I'll do anything you want, just speak. Just speak again. To me.* And then—he spoke to me again, smiling, but he spoke only in Italian, and I knew hardly a word. How awful....

Awful. We had no language in common—and yet it didn't matter, I could understand him. We walked for hours in the hot Italian sun. All I remember now, is how I felt. Melted, destroyed, done for —*don't laugh at me, you bloody fool, every woman wants to feel like that. Once, at least. Once, at least, in her life.* As I write these words, I am playing Puccini on my Sony. No, I am not a fool, I know exactly what I am doing. Now. How I wish I could go back now, as I am now. That can never be, that we are not allowed to do....

At dusk we ended up on the steps of a cathedral. The dying light of day was soft butter gold, the piazza was awash in gold light. There were fireflies, I had never seen fireflies before. A dozen of his friends, young men and boys, were sitting on the stone steps of the cathedral playing guitars and singing Neapolitan love songs. Love songs! All of Italy is a stereotype, so help me. His sister was there on the cathedral steps, singing Verdi! I am remembering, I am sitting on the steps of a cathedral in the Mezzogiorno, in gold light, I am sixteen years old and the air is full of song, I am dying, thinking *Salvatore, Salvatore, what now, what do you want with me, you know you can do whatever you want, say something. Please, Salvatore, just say words I can understand, say Something....* And Salvatore said, "Mia Mama, you come?"

Would you like to come and meet my mother? And I was suddenly stone sober. Meet Salvatore's mother? No. No, that was not what I wanted to do. I thought to myself, *No, Salvatore, I think I know what I want to do with you now, and it is not to go and meet your mother. No. Not at all.*

"Salvatore, not now, I am tired, I need to rest. My hotel room is only ten minutes from here. I just today bought a very special bottle of liqueur, it is not even open yet. Will you come with me and taste it with me?" Salvatore was happy to come with me and do as I wished, and I had my way. His mama? Maybe there *was* no mama. Perhaps, God help me, there was a gentle mother, and dinner waiting, and a universe of kindness. I did not want kindness, I did not want mother. I wanted Salvatore. We went to my room. We sipped my liqueur— which was not really liqueur, it was a bottle of superb Pantelleria Muscato. We sat on the edge of my bed and talked, and then—please forgive me I am trying to tell the simple truth. For two hours we broke on each other.

I have never been as happy, before or since. I have never been so tired or so alive, or so convinced of the joy of being alive on God's earth; and then I fell into deepest unconsciousness. Salvatore came with me, I know he did. Don't ask, I don't know how, but I know he did come with me. We lay together floating on our backs, looking up at the infinite stars above the roof, and we slept. Salvatore awoke first.

I came awake in the darkness and couldn't, for a brief moment, remember where I was or how I had come; then memories flooded back. A wave of sheer pleasure washed over me. I reached out on the dark bed to touch this beautiful human being who now belonged to me and I touched nothing. (My flesh crawls as I write these words)... Sleepily I flailed my arm further across the bed. It was empty. Where has he gone, why? Of course, he has gone to the toilet. No. Now my sleep-stunned brain is beginning to function. He *is* gone. A premonition: He is gone, really gone, *what else...?* I leapt off the bed, groped for a light switch, could not find it in the black of night, then found it. Bright light. And, my brain crawling in disbelief, I took inventory.

—Salvatore was gone, and his clothes with him.
    —*Destitution*
—My wallet was gone, and with it my money and my credit cards. My ring and gold chain also gone.
    —*Betrayal*
—The Muscato? The SOB took my Muscato!
    — *Insult*
—My passport! He left me my passport.
    Good of him; he didn't have an easy way to sell it.

But oh, Salvatore, Salvatore, what about the gifts you couldn't take for profit and instead destroyed? Oh Salvatore, the trust you had from me and never knew, and now no man will ever know....

Years later, I told the story of Salvatore to a few women I thought were friends, and two of them said fiercely, "*I want to meet that man.*" Why would anyone freely choose to drink VINO DEL CASA rather than late harvest? And yet..... Life nevertheless is very beautiful. You *must try* the Muscato of Panetelleria. We recommend especially the Late, Late Harvest—it is particularly sweet.

AN ORDINARY DAY IN ISTANBUL

*A*mong the great cities of the Mediterranean, some are museums simply feeding upon the riches of their past. Venice is the perfect example, drunk on its magnificent history. Others, such as Marseille, boil with the vitality of the present day; to these cities one goes in search of life. But in the greatest city of them all, Istanbul, the past and present are so intimately interwoven as to be a single fabric. On an ordinary day in Istanbul, past and present wrap around one another as do the bodies of lovers. They curl back upon one another like a dog nibbling on its own tail, or the new moon tracking the old. On an ordinary day in Istanbul yesterday and today may, in fact, be nearly indistinguishable. Let me give you an example. Suppose I go to visit a friend in her shop....

Turkan is one of the lovelier women in Istanbul, where there are a million beautiful women. She is short, seductive, comical, and her warm brown face is straight out of Central Asia. However, Turkan is a woman of mood swings; on one morning laughter and euphoria pour out of her, but on the next she may be in depression. On this particular morning she was sitting at her desk at the family business just off Istiklal Caddesi and dripping pathos on the plate glass. Her shoulders were rounded, her body slumped forward, and clearly the future was grim.

"I saw my doctor last night, it is as I thought; I have a disease. My life is ruined." Turkan dripped self-pity, she was despair incarnate. Quiet despair. It is all over, she is done for....

"What disease?" I asked.

"I can't tell you." A rather long pause followed.

"So.   That means it is a sexually transmitted disease."

"Yes. How did you know?"

"What disease is it?"

"It is terrible. I can't tell you. My life is ruined. Now, no man will ever want me. I will never have children. (Pause.) It is a virus disease."

"Is it called herpes?"

"Yes." She stares. "How did you know?"

This is a matter of simple probability. I ignored the question. "So, what's the problem? What else is new?"

"*Don't you hear? My life is ruined.* I will never have a husband or children, men will not even want to love me. I am done for. And my father does not even know I am not a virgin."

I think I will not participate in this tragedy. I am not in the mood. "Turkan, you are right on one count. In about sixty years you will be dead, and that will definitely ruin your life. So, correct: some day your life is ruined. As to the rest, all of the men in Istanbul would make love to you; a great many—including me—would marry you. And a great many men and women have this virus, including me. After a month or two, you will see it is no more serious than a bad cold."

"You have it?"

"Yes."

"I don't understand. You don't have protruding canine fangs or green saliva (I paraphrase) but you have *herpes*? But you seem like such a nice man." She thinks for a moment. "But I know I will never find a husband."

"Turkan, I will marry you tomorrow."

"But you are too old to make children."

"Turkan, I may be old but I am not too old to be insulted! To this insult I say what a young man in the villages would say to you. In three months you will be with child; then you *are* ruined, then you must quickly marry me. In the night your mother will kill a chicken. In the morning we hang the sheet, with the blood, on the porch railing. Then you are saved! You were a virgin, now you have a husband and soon a baby, you are already beautiful, rich, famous and terribly funny. What else do you want from life?"

"You are too old, if only you were thirty-five."

"I have ten very good years left. Then you can poison me, and grab another. In America this is what they do. In America everyone will want you! Your whole life is ahead of you!"

After perhaps a half hour of this despair and hand-wringing, we have a mood swing. Turkan feels much better. Now she is flirtatious. "I feel much better. You are such a nice man. I can talk to you. Maybe my life is not ruined after all." There is a pause, and then, "Would you like to go to a football game tonight? It is on the Asian side." Yes, I would like to. "It is very expensive, about $30. And we will be there from eight until midnight." No. I change my mind. Four hours? Midnight?

"Why is it so expensive, Turkan?"

"We would need seats in a small covered section, it is the only place where girls are allowed." Why? "Because everywhere else there are men, and they are cussing, the girls should not hear this. Of course," and now Turkan pauses for thought, "of course, the girls curse worse than the men..." We go on to other subjects and then she says,

"Would you like to go to a French restaurant with me tonight? (The football is now out of mind.) It is the best restaurant in Istanbul, a great view of the Bosphorus, very expensive. I will take you. I made a lot of money today, we sold an apartment house. Would you like? I pick you up with taxi tonight at 7:30 pm!"

The air is thick with superlatives: very beautiful girl, very good restaurant, a great view of the magnificent Bosphorus, with glittering palaces and ships under a perfectly timed, very golden full moon. And she is buying. I think about all the other things I had planned, like going to bed at 9:30 pm ....

"Yes, Turkan, I would like that." Oh, very yes.

We sat on a hilltop overlooking the stunning glitter of the Bosphorus until nearly midnight, talking and watching the lights of the two great suspension bridges, the myriad boats and ships. We sat like lords over the great waterway and each drank a couple of Margueritas. Then, along with many courses of food, we killed a splendid bottle of red wine, and part of another. The service was very French, the food was more Turkish, and very good—although I can cook a better lamb. I must confess that during the evening I lapsed briefly into a vile act. In a degenerate moment I smoked one of Turkan's cigarettes, the first in about thirty years. She didn't seem to notice; she is a normal Turk and smoked most of the pack herself.

Under a high and quiet sky, the ships passed back and forth: businesslike, plodding tankers down from the Caucasus; fish-boats from Sariyer carrying the day's catch to the City; tourist tour-boats all a-glitter with strings of jewels. Sailing yachts, tugs, freighters, a fire-boat, perhaps the Polisi. And slowly, after we moved to the outside deck for coffee, that vast gold moon rose over Anatolia just as it has since the first Greeks came here 3300 years ago, just as it has since we were all young and the world was new, and the Greeks came here to make Byzantium. Then the Romans came to make Constantinople, City of the Heart's Desire— which also quickly became Greek. And the Turks came, and made Istanbul. The City—broken over and over again, and never broken. Sooner or later the Mongols came, and the Arabs came, and the Venetians came—oh yes, about the Venetians.

The Byzantines started it all. A thousand years ago a functionary from this very city appointed the first Doge of Venice. And for years the Venetians came as traders to the city; but always they came with envy, and with mixed or hostile feelings, and perhaps with greed in their hearts, for this was by far the richest and most important city in the Western world. Finally, in 1204 AD the Venetians brought the Fourth Crusade here to rape and loot the city, the first of two death blows to the Byzantines. Soon the Turks came with the second.

As Turkan and I sat over our coffee on the sparkling Bosphorus that night, we could see a few kilometers to the north the lights of the second Bosphorus bridge. At that narrow strait of the Bosphorus, the choke-point, the Turks many years ago built two powerful forts: On the European side, Rumeli Hisari; on the Asian side, Anadolu Hisari. They were military, of course, but they were also the primary tax collectors for all shipping up and down the waterway. And whenever I think of them, I think about the day a Venetian captain decided to ignore the taxes. Now, the Venetian hates taxes as much as any man alive. Given a choice between a tax bill and a deadly disease .... a Venetian would think about it. This particular ship came down the

Bosphorus under full sail, flying like a bat. He dropped a few sails as he approached the lee of Rumeli Hisari, hinting at a stop - and then suddenly ran them back up. As he flew past, the cannon of the angry Turks first demasted and then sank the unfortunate trader. The Venetians swam ashore, most of them, where the Turks lined them up and beheaded them, one at a time. Except for the last one. I have always imagined this last unfortunate soul standing on a miserable Turkish shoreline, his bowels long since evacuated in terror, and now facing a Turkish officer—who is making a speech:

"My dear fellow, we Turks are a hospitable people, a warm-hearted people. I am sure you have drunk with us in the taverns of Galata, enjoyed the whores of Galata. I am sure you know we are a gentle people. But when the Greeks think of us, they think of pyramids of skulls, and we have our reputation to maintain. We are warriors - and you Venetians are shopkeepers and tax evaders, beneath the lowliest cleaners of toilets. Please deliver this piece of paper to your Doge; you are free to go. Take the next ship departing to the West." And the Turk handed the wretched Venetian a tax bill, due on that same exact date.

Back in the present, over breakfast at my pension the following morning, I summarized my quite enjoyable evening to a friend. And he wanted to know more about the Venetian ships.

"You didn't make that up, did you? Where did you get that story?"

"Sir! I never make things up. Don't insult me. I *think* that story was in Mansel's *Constantinople*. I am going to the Sahaflar Carsisi, the book bazaar, in a few minutes. If you want to come with me, we can look for it. Do you know the Sahaflar Carsisi? It is full of beautiful history and lovely people. Come with me...."

We went to the book bazaar, to the shop of a dear friend. We searched unsuccessfully for the reference. It was there somewhere, but I couldn't find it. Shortly my breakfast companion went on his way, and I settled down to drink tea with the shop owner. Usually this heavy, jolly, intellectual woman was full of good cheer. Not now. Suddenly I saw that she was nearly in tears, she could barely hold up her head.

"Meltem, what in heaven is wrong? You look so sad."

"I saw my doctor last night, it is as I thought; I have an illness .... I am ruined."

"What disease?"

"I can't tell you. But... my life is done for, it is all over...."?

"Meltem, is it a virus disease?"

"No. Allah, why would you ask such a question? No, no, it is my heart. I had much pain, the doctor says it is just stress, but I know better. My life is ruined...."

"What is all the stress, Meltem, what is that about? If you want to tell me."

"All right, I will tell you. My family had a huge tax bill to pay—from our business—and we tried to avoid paying. We are caught, we will lose everything. Tax evasion. I will be destitute. *I am done for. If I am poor, my life is ruined. No man will want me, I will never have a husband or children... I think I am losing my head."*

I shall not participate in this tragedy. Now I know what to say to the sweet woman. "Meltem, let us talk this over. And then let us go out for a good dinner tonight. You will feel better. Perhaps some place over the Bosphorus.... Do you have any money left?"

MADIHA: A BEGGAR GIRL

*I*n the Third World, beauty does not save a girl from the gutter. There are too many girls and too many gutters. This girl might have been twenty, she had a healthy infant in her lap, she sat on the grimy streets of Alexandria in her worn and dirty clothes—and when she smiled she was absolutely stunning. The smile was haunting. The first time I gave her a half pound, and she looked only at my face—and smiled. The second time I gave her three pounds. A pound was about thirty cents, with several times the value in local foodstuffs. The third time she waved from across the street— warmly, as if to a friend—and I crossed over gave her ten pounds. Each time she looked right in my eyes, smiling, and not at the money. The last time, I patted her shoulder. As I left, a man fifty feet away quietly said "Thank you" as I passed. I wished I could talk to her, but assumed we did not share a language. However, the next time we met her soft voice said, "What is your name?" She had spoken in hesitant, broken, but quite understandable English.

I told her my name.

"Where you from?"

"Do you have children?"

"Why you stay in Alexandria so long?"

"I see you here long time.... You like Alex? Yes...."

"Why you give me so much money? You have a good heart, Allah looks very kindly on you. Thank you..."   And as I answered her questions, I saw her become shy....

"And you?" I asked her. "Your name?"

"Madiha."

Then, realizing that we could talk, and I might ask her anything at all, I decided to learn more.

"How old are you?"

"Seventeen."

"How did you learn to speak English?"

"I go to school only three years. Mostly I talk to other kids who go school. I not read...."

"You have a husband? Baby's father?"

"No man takes care of me like husband."

"You have mother here, father?"

"Mother is dead. Father there."

She pointed down the street at an older man. It was the man who had said "Thank you" yesterday.

"Your father watches over you?"

"Father take care of me. The money I get, we eat that. It is only the three of us."

"Why did you leave the land?"

"My father... he think life will be better in city. Maybe it is. My baby not die of the diseases.... But always think about the Nile. Nile is more kind than Alex."

"Can I ask you one question?" she asked.

"Yes, of course."

"What is it, what you call happiness? Chase of happiness? In America you say that."

"Pursuit of happiness." I tried to imagine how to answer.

"How can you chase that? As if you chase down an animal...."

"Chase, pursuit, not the right words, you are right."

"Then tell me right. I want to understand America. But you talk as if is an amount of a thing."

"Yes. You are right. We talk like that."

"Like amount of water in glass."

"Yes."

"Not right idea."

"No."

"I don't know 'happiness.' You tell me, I don't understand. 'This day ok,' yes, I know. Joy, yes. Sad, yes. Not *happiness*."

"I'm sorry, I don't know how to tell you."

"Why?"

"I just don't know how."

"You don't know happiness?"

"No, I don't know happiness."

"You talk about this, you don't have it?"

"No."

"Can you find it? Do you make it? Somebody else make it?"

"Well, we talk about making somebody else happy, but...."

"How you make? You can make me happy? I make you?"

"You can't make me happy. Except for a moment when you smile." She smiled widely, pleased, and then said,

"Can make *me* happy?"

At that moment I said stupid things, things I wish terribly I could call back. "I could—or someone could— help you go to school, help you to leave the street, wear clean things, have things for your baby." In an instant she was hurt and angry, and the smile drained from her face.

"Madiha give you the dirty clothes, baby for to beg. Then you happy?"

"No."

"I take away your school. You happy?"

"No."

"I take your money, your clothes, things. Then you will be happy?"

"No."

"*Why you think that I happy if you change me?* Allah give me baby, father, Nile not far away, maybe I go back. Allah give me smile you like. Is all what I know. I have joy, good heart. Not enough? I not want you things. Allah enough."

"I'm sorry, I'm so sorry I said what I said."

"Americans happy?"

"I think— some yes, some no."

"I think you not truth. I look in eyes of Americans, French, English. Good clothes. Money. Most look away from me, don't give like Allah say to give. When I look in their eyes, behind eyes mostly I see ruins. Desert. Desert like beyond the Nile. No happy."

"I think... I think you are right. We hunt, we pursue something, we don't know when we find it. You are right, we pursue happiness as if it were the amount of water in a glass. An amount."

"Now I think I understand, American. I have idea when you talk about glass of water. Egypt glass of water—is the Nile. But fellahin not measure amount of water in the Nile like you. We don't measure of water. Exact amount in glass—in Nile—not matter. Only thing matters is enough flood each year for the land. And very terrible if Nile very high, very low. You Americans want more and more in glass. You want flood. Fellahin happy—yes, maybe right word—if Nile half full. We okay if glass half full. Half empty, no difference, still okay. We can tell—is enough."

A silence followed and stretched out into many moments.... I had no words worth the saying. She was done. All I could do was sit there on my heels and wait. After a little while she allowed a smile to creep back on her face. Maybe, a smile of satisfaction. She knew she had done for me. Finally I spoke.

"Madiha, about the sad things I said... I'm very sorry. This is not to make it okay. But, here—" I put 50 pounds in her lap. She smiled in my eyes, looked down, smiled again. And she said,

"Suk'ran. Is more than I get all day. You are kind man. How long you stay in Alex?"

"I leave tomorrow," I said.

"Sorry. Maybe not see you later. You good to me. So I tell you a secret." Her smile widened, her eyes twinkled. "Madiha and father have 3,000 pounds in bank! Maybe near $1000 American! It is enough...."

A MATTER OF GRACE

The restaurant was four or five blocks back from the quay of the Old Port in a neighborhood that had seen its best days before the invention of the airplane. Once it had been comfortable, residential; now it was the home of the poor, the Algerian, the eccentric, and the man or woman whose occupation is not to be discussed without good reason. For days I had asked the French of Marseille for a restaurant offering decent and inexpensive food, and a patron who spoke at least a few words of English. By word, by tone and by facial expression, the answers came clean and emphatic: "You are a fool to ask for both decent and cheap. To ask also for English, you are clearly American and mad." Finally, however, heavily dusted with Gallic scorn, I found a place that apparently satisfied my needs.

I am not permitted to name the restaurant, for reasons presently obvious, but it was an informal and attractive place with perhaps twenty tables. Above the restaurant, I eventually learned, were a dozen or so comfortable hotel rooms. The place had a vague air of elegance, but the significance of a soft and delicate interior, an expensive 18th century print or two on the walls—all this went sailing over my head. The manager was a heavyset and quiet woman who might have been sixty. Madame was distantly cordial, and perhaps a little surprised or amused that I had found the place; it was, after all, in a dubious neighborhood in a city of dubious reputation. But Madame was cordial until I began to inquire the prices of wines and entrees. Then, abruptly she was annoyed. "You should not ask of price here, nor should you need to. How much can you spend for the evening? Very well. You are here, it is a slow evening, it would amuse me to talk with an American. Don't ask again of the cost. Don't bother to order. I will take care of it all." And she did.

The meal Madame put before me, the wines brought by a beautiful and unobtrusive waitress, were simply the finest I shall ever have in my life. As I think back, I don't know which is the more remarkable—the superb quality of that remarkable gift of food and drink, or the fact that it was all nameless. I was not told what I ate or drank; Madame was occupied while I ate, and the waitress simply came, smiled and left. A feast fit for anyone on earth, but nameless. So strange.... Then Madame came and casually sat at my table, and we exchanged the small remarks that pass the time of evening. And I could not longer contain my curiosity. I took the chance that this confident woman accepted challenges, and I asked her straight out: "How do you come to be here with this lovely place—in the slums of Marseille? How is it you speak perfect standard American English, and lack the usual Gallic contempt for my country? Who are you?" Madame stared casually into my eyes, and I could almost hear her mind asking, *Should I bother, should I not?* And then—this is the story she told.

You asked earlier if a room was available. Tonight I have empty rooms, you can have #8 upstairs. Now, I will answer your questions, it amuses me occasionally to tell how I came here. But on this condition: the man who sent you here did it as a joke. Fine. You found me in a good mood, and I gift you. But tomorrow you leave and do not return.

I was born in Marseille, very near here, but by 1945 the war had made life difficult and I was a prostitute on the streets of Paris. I was in every way ordinary, but I was young and had the natural beauty of the young. Early one evening on the streets of Paris an American army officer spoke to me—I spoke a little English—and I chatted, waiting for him to do business. I was obviously dressed as a whore, but in a few minutes this man very respectfully asked to buy me a dinner. I shrugged. In 1945 one accepted all gifts.

He bought me a very expensive dinner, treated me with great respect, and by the time we had eaten I am thinking—*How annoying, this nice stupid man has not yet realized I am a whore. If only I were decently dressed.* But this is a very dumb American, he *never* realized. I am expecting to pay him for the dinner with the bed—and very respectfully he asked to "see me" again tomorrow night. "Yes, of course," I said, "but now I must go." I made him leave the restaurant first, so that he would not see the bottom of my bottom as I fled. He never saw me in the clothes of a prostitute again, you can be sure. That evening, once rid of the American, I worked the streets. But in a different neighborhood. When I met James the next evening—that was his name —I was in gorgeous borrowed clothes. He was even more respectful, he wanted to see me again the following evening, and each evening for a week. He was never touching me. Hardly even kissed me. I have called James stupid, for he was very naive, but in fact I was no better. Each night, in war-shattered France, I was eating better than I had ever imagined in my life. I stuffed myself joyfully, and sat passively to see what the man would do next.... and then the bottom fell out of my world. James asked me to marry him.

I, a seventeen-year-old, half-literate prostitute from the slums of Marseille? I was to marry this rich American soldier and go with him to some place called Oklahoma? God knows, what is Oklahoma? Sure, James, I will marry you. Sure—you are a nice man, you will be kind, I love you not at all, but you are rich and I am poor—a poor whore. I will marry you and have an American passport. And we will see what happens. But, I thought silently, cynically, be assured I do not love you. I love my cat. But I do not love you, for I have no idea who you are. I shall take you—as gently as possible, I am not cruel—but I shall take you. Now, long after, how my heart laughs at the thought! I did not do any such thing, for James deserved nothing of the kind. I set one condition on the marriage. "James, if I marry you, you can afford to let me come back for a little while each summer to see my family and friends? Otherwise I shall die of loneliness. Your Oklahoma will be very foreign to me. Okay?" And James happily agreed. Yes, he said, he could afford to do that. Hah!

Three months later we were driving from a place called Oklahoma City to a place called Enid under a warm, high and vast sky, a sky such as I had never, never imagined. Against a fierce blue light never seen in Paris, great masses of white cumulus clouds marched boiling and spilling across a sky so high... so high... unspeakable, incomprehensible. Violent electrical storms marched on endless plains. I found a gentle town never touched by war. Naive kind people. A loving family. A simple, unsophisticated, lonely town of warm, kind, kind people. I was taken to a splendid Victorian farmhouse full of luxury—and told

I was to rule over it. One insanity after another. I was a Paris whore, a whore, what am I doing? What am I doing here? And the final shock soon came. James said, "Let's take a drive, and I will show you our land." I thought he meant, "show you some of Oklahoma."

We drove for what seemed several kilometers and made a right turn; it was all straight lines and right angles, how boring, under that dumbfounding high sky. We drove around a rectangle many kilometers on a side. James pulled back into our driveway. Stopped, turned off the ignition. Looked over at me with a casual smile, and said, "What do you think of our land?" WHAT THE ____! WHAT DO YOU MEAN, OUR LAND? James explained, at some length. He had just driven around ten sections of the finest wheat and oil land in northwest Oklahoma. It was what we—*he kept saying we*—owned. In our own name. His father owned far more. I was married to the only son of one of the wealthiest families in northwest Oklahoma. I was in way over my head, and I finally knew it. Mother of God, what had I done....?

The rest of the story I will cut short. I saw finally that I had married a very decent and good man who also happened to be very rich. Jimmy was a good man, so I decided to love him. The love of respect, not of passion. I learned excellent English. I served him well and gave him and my own selfish little self four beautiful sons and a lovely daughter. In the process I grew up. I became far more than what I had been when Jimmy found me. We stayed together thirty-five years, until he died. The man gave me great gifts, and I made him a very good wife. Was I bored? In Oklahoma? Not at all, I held Jimmy to our agreement. Each June and July for thirty-five years, even when I was pregnant, I returned to be with all my friends. In Paris. And, of course, in Paris I worked, but now in an upper-class brothel. Oh, you are surprised? Of course I jest, I knew you would be shocked. You Americans never understand anything. When I am in Oklahoma I see to it the ashtrays are clean. When I deal with the men in Paris, sometimes I drink champagne from the ashtray— or, to exaggerate a little, I may throw it at the man! It is the excitement, the passion, the laughter, the simple fact of being *alive*! The money? I spent it on valuable clothes for my wonderful husband. Did he find out? So far as I could discover, no one in Oklahoma knew the difference between a $20 scarf and a $200 scarf. Not one. Jimmy was the best dressed man in Oklahoma, and I was the only one who knew.

In the end my husband died. I divided most of our wealth among our four sons. I returned to Paris to find that I had become old—in the mind, not just the body. The body really is not important. So I returned to the home of my childhood, this poor section of Marseille, and opened my establishment. Now, monsieur, I weary of this, if you will excuse me. The last question? Who am I? I shall answer that in the morning. You have #8. If you will excuse me—

"Who am I? Monsieur, do you not think I have already given the answer? Have I not entertained you sufficiently?" We stood on the bottom steps in front of the little restaurant, I had finished with my thanks for Madame's gifts. For a lovely evening and a deeply quiet night, madame had refused any payment whatever. "After all, monsieur, have I not told you the story of my life, my entertaining past? Does not this answer the question, Who am I?"

"But no, Madame." (Rest assured I was smiling gently, we parted cordially). "But no, you yourself just conceded that you have told me the wonderful story of your *past*. With all respect and admiration, my dear Madame, who are you *now*?"

"Very well, Monsieur, I concede the point. Now... now I am the owner of the most exclusive brothel in Marseille. But do not concern yourself Monsieur, everything is done with grace." As she said these words Madame was standing one step above me on the stairway of the restaurant. She looked down at me with an extremely sardonic smile. And with her old eyes glittering like a sky full of stars, she added, "If you were ever to see my establishment, Monsieur, you probably would not even recognize it for what it is. It is a matter of grace."

In growing awareness and shock, I stared back at the woman and reflexly, intensely objected. "Madame, *this* cannot be your establishment. During our very enjoyable conversations last evening, you introduced me to a beautifully dressed young woman you said was your daughter! She spoke with me briefly. She *behaved* as your daughter. *This cannot be your establishment.*"

Madame was now impatient; her voice was short, and her words were to the point. "This is indeed my establishment. Anne is indeed my daughter, back from the University for a brief vacation. So? Everyone here knows her. Everyone here is civilized. Also, they all know that anyone who offends her is a dead man." She paused, her face softened a bit and she nearly smiled. Then she added a final remark.

"We would never have to do that, of course. But if we did, it would be done right. *Don't you understand? Can't you understand? It is all a matter of grace. It is all ... simply ... a matter of grace.*"

THE MARKET ECONOMY:
A PARABLE IN DIVERSE PARTS

The essentials of trade have been the same for thousands of years, perhaps ever since the world began. First, you must know what I have to sell. Perhaps you walk past my shop in a bazaar in Turkey or Lebanon, and I offer you a gift: a sample of my cheese, or apricots, or almonds. You did not know you were going to buy almonds today? You did not know that I have the best almonds in the world—and cheap? Now we have a market. The second essential is trust; all good trade is repeat trade, only pirates deal but once. So I treat you fairly, and you return. And the last essential is to establish a fair price for the goods; to this end we shall negotiate, bargain. Given demand, trust, and an agreed value for the product, we have established trade. In order to make these universal principles quite clear, we offer several examples involving very different kinds of merchandise.

I — General Merchandise
The Phoenicians were the first great trading empire of the Mediterranean. They entered history in the 16th century BC and were dominant in maritime trade from 1100 to 700 BC; they were the first to trade over the entire Mediterranean and into the Atlantic. By the 6th century they had circumnavigated Africa, the first to do so. Writing in the 5th century, Herodotus described their trading practices on the Atlantic coast of Africa —

probably in modern-day Morocco, and probably in such as cloth, glass, dyes, spices, silver and other metals, ivory, and light manufactured goods and foodstuffs (oil, honey):

> "They trade with a race of men who live in a part of Libya beyond the Pillars of Heracles. On reaching this country, they unload their goods, arrange them tidily along the beach, and then, returning to their boats, raise a smoke. Seeing the smoke, the natives come down to the beach, place on the ground a certain quantity of gold in exchange for the goods, and go off again to a distance. The Carthaginians then come ashore and take a look at the gold; and if they think it represents a fair price for their wares, they collect it and go away; if, on the other hand, it seems too little, they go back aboard and wait, and the natives come and add to the gold until they are satisfied. There is perfect honesty on both sides; the Carthaginians never touch the gold until it equals in value what they have offered for sale, and the natives never touch the goods until the gold has been taken away...."

Parenthetically, in the ancient world any meeting between previously isolated peoples was fraught with danger not only from hostilities, but perhaps especially from unfamiliar diseases. To trade on the beach, with little or no physical contact, was the almost perfect solution.

II—A Slave

In a hilarious story dating from 1843, the French traveler Gerard de Nerval tells of moving into a rented house in a respectable neighborhood of Cairo—only to be informed by authorities that he must leave within days unless he takes into his home either a wife or a female slave. A French bachelor living alone is a menace to a proper Muslim neighborhood, and a sixty year old widow has complained! Nerval's Egyptian friend advises him to convert to Islam and marry immediately. Non? Then—to the slave market. In a comic opera of cultural differences, Nerval and Abdullah go shopping in the slave bazaars. Nerval was scorned by certain slaves recommended by Abdullah. He rejected others. Without bargaining, and with little or no idea of the "value" of these women, Nerval eventually bought a spectacularly beautiful girl of Javanese Hindi origins with a challenging name: Z't'n'b. The pronunciation was something like "Zetnaybia," overlain by a sneeze.

Zetnaybia, once in her new home, immediately made it quite clear *she would neither cook nor sew nor clean*, but that on the contrary Nerval should now return to the markets and buy a slave for her. Zetnaybia made it clear that under Islamic law she had many rights, and was really not born to be a drudge; in fact, she was more like an exotic but useless adopted child. Months later Nerval announced that he was leaving for Lebanon, and that he was giving Zetnaybia the gift of freedom. She became hysterical; this would tell the world she was worthless, a slave of no value, and she would be a derelict in the Cairo slums. Please, she begged, take me back and resell me (to a better master, to be sure!) Eventually, after much cost and comic entertainment, Nerval left his "slave" happily placed in a French convent in Lebanon. *At his cost.* Beware of markets where one is ignorant of the merchandise, the costs and the values.

III—Copper Pots

Not many years ago, all over the Mediterranean coastlines, a nearly identical comedy was repeated over and over again. The wife had thrown an old and oft-patched copper cooking pot into a corner of the kitchen. Soon it would be thrown on the back yard trash heap. An American tourist—or perhaps she was English or German—happened to see the pot, and remarked,

"That is a nice old pot." Perhaps the tourist even said, "Would you sell it to me?" The old Italian housewife—or perhaps she was Greek or Turk or French—was not so stupid, and replied in a bored voice,

"How much do you want to pay?"

"$25?"

"TWENTY-FIVE DOLLARS? Let us bargain together. (That is not so much, however....)" Soon, for twenty miles around, old women were digging up the last two hundred years of their trash heaps. Soon they discovered, emptying their cupboards, that:

Junk copper pots brought $25.

However, "ANTIQUES" sold for $50, and

"ANTIQUITIES" brought $100, or $300!

And an entire new and previously unimaginable trade was born. The old mothers learned many new words, such as ANTIK. And they learned about "advertising."

IV—Souvenirs & Girls

With the collapse of the USSR, a growing flood of free-enterprise traders poured south into Istanbul from

Russia, the Ukraine, Georgia, Romania and Bulgaria. Many were young and middle-aged women. Many carried suitcases, either empty or containing an assortment of cheap carved wooden trinkets, valuable icons and family treasures, wartime relics, and junk. These they sold on the streets of Istanbul, returning north with suitcases filled with cheap, low-quality clothes for resale. To the Turks most of these women are Russians and Girls, and their commerce is called the Suitcase Trade. A story circulates in Istanbul that one day, not long after this suitcase trade began, a beautiful Russian girl stood on a Galata street selling trinkets for perhaps a dollar each, and was approached by a nice looking young Turk. He bargained over the souvenirs, and then said an unexpected thing. With a gentle smile, he said,

"Your souvenirs are a dollar. I will give you ten dollars to spend the night with me." If the man had appeared ugly or unkind, who knows? As it was, perhaps the girl looked back at him, remembered her crowded little hotel room, her tired back, and thought to herself, Nice little fool you are, I would have done it for free. And she said,

"Sure. Will you buy me a dinner too?"

The story I have heard—surely a foolishness, but an interesting one—is that in the Russian suitcase trade of Istanbul, a one-to-ten ratio was established. A year later the trinkets were $3, the girls were $30. Within approximately four years, free-market forces reached an equilibrium that exists to this day. The best junk is $10, it is said, and the most desirable girls are $100 per night (always there can be bargaining.) Herodotus wrote something to the effect that in the Libyan desert there are camels with tails like a fish—if you would believe a Libyan.

V—Tragedy

There is a "rule" in physics that says, *That which is not forbidden is compulsory.* In other words: *if a thing can happen, it will happen.* (If not yet, then later.) Once upon a time on the shores of the Mediterranean there lived a tired, poor old woman with nine children. Her husband had abandoned her. Her youngest child, a little girl of three, happened to be a little lame and perhaps a little homely and simple, but this child had a sweet smile. When the little girl smiled it was as if all the blessings in the world had condensed into one great blaze of light. Lame, homely, simple—but inside, an angel. And then, one day a tourist—perhaps also a little lame and simple —saw this child smile, saw the mother in her misery mistreat her little girl, and the tourist said,

"I see you don't like this little girl. You really don't want her, do you? Would you consider letting me...."

And the tired old mother, knowing not what she did, perhaps just to get rid of the stupid tourist who was wasting her day, said,

"How much would you....?"

And all over the shores of the Mediterranean....

I include this nonsense because I once watched a beautiful little girl repeatedly abused by an unhappy mother in a small port town. When I idly remarked to an older woman resident that I wished I could buy the child, adopt her, take her away—the response was a savage, "She would sell her."

Aye, and what then?

Woman in a Black Mask

*I*magine for a moment that all of this, all we experience, is similar to an infinite hotel corridor going on into the distance. We walk forever down an infinite carpet, and every fifteen feet or so on both sides there are doors. Some of them stand wide open. Others are open only a few inches, perhaps with a chain across the gap. Some doors are closed. Some locked. And some are triple dead-bolted. Perhaps each door is a person, each moment a new door. In fact... in fact the doors are real and time is not. The only thing is, we don't see it.

On a plane to Madrid, Harrison Ford was having a lot of fairly complicated trouble with a married but pretty blonde on a Hawaiian beach. The movie script guaranteed that it would end well, but it doesn't have to be like that. Usually there is no script hanging on the door.

Why do we knock on all the closed doors, the empty rooms? Are we afraid of those that open? Is there an abyss beyond? Perhaps it is like the emergency exit doors on this airliner.... As I write these words we are at 33,000' somewhere over the Atlantic, and we do not think about opening the doors. We do not even see them as doors, not really. If we did that, we would all remember that we are going to die—and that would change everything.

The fox watched the hawk
the hawk watched the fox
.... we were both watching.

Venice. Carnevale. A small out-of-the-way piazza
near Cattedrali Frari. And here a band of richly
costumed actors and dancers made the Carnevale.
They played, danced, and finally completed the
performance. And at the end she was standing on the
other side of the piazza with the milling band of
theatricals between us— a woman in a black mask. She
wore a formal deep purple evening gown fit for a grand
ball, tight-waited and decorated with white trim. Deep
neckline, short sleeves. A large white feather decorated
the front of the gown, another plume stood jauntily
from her hat. She had slender white arms. And wore a
wig of flowing white curls, and a black mask.
    The performance ended. The woman was fierce.
Staring at her, I began to move to my right. Instantly
she saw, and mirrored me, moving to her left. She
didn't miss a thing. When empty space lay between us,
we walked slowly up to each other, mirror images.
What she saw, I do not know. Years later, when asked,
she told someone my eyes were daggers. We spoke
briefly, exchanged names. (Ristin). Addresses
(Norwegian). Then she was gone, an apparition in a
velvet gown, a white wig and a black mask. I never saw
her face. She could have been twenty or fifty, beautiful
or ugly, kind or cruel. What was there—all that one
could see through the mask—was that fierce aliveness
staring through a narrow crack in an open door. The
eyes were real.

    Two and a half years later, we met at the airport in
Sevilla and went South.

On the Andelusian beach at sunset,
  horses.
Longline fisherboats sliding into the sea.
In the dying light, egrets and terns.
On the sand a lean, solitary man,
  emaciated, a savage
brown hatchet face, a throwing net,
the weights dangling from one shoulder.
Bats in the dusk and glitter of Tangier.
  Africa.
The Phoenicians came here in peace, trading.
The Romans salted tuna back of the beach
before Christ. But then for a thousand years
this place was a war-strait: Gibraltar,
Choke-point for Arab armies
  Spanish frigates,
  English cannon,
  sails of Moorish pirates,
  others.
Nothing changes here, the world simply
  repeats itself.
At sunset a Norwegian woman
  walked on the beach—
  in both of her hands,
  Smiles.

As soon as we know we are going to die,
  then there is the possibility to be alive.

THE SACRIFICE

Figan and Ismet Cok live in a quiet, comfortable apartment in the southern fringe of Ankara. They are both highly respected university faculty, and probably represent everything characteristic and admirable about modern, Western-oriented secular Turkey. They are also marvelously warm-hearted friends. Their apartment is beautifully furnished, and includes most of the modern conveniences: television, CD and video players, word-processor, fax, E-mail, all the usual kitchen appliances. A few days before my first visit in 1996 my dear friends had purchased a new, deep red Toyota Corolla. However, during the first week of my visit Figan and Ismet casually remarked, more than once, that, "perhaps we will sacrifice a sheep on Sunday." Suspecting that perhaps I was the butt of some sort of joke, I glanced humorously about my surroundings. I could see no sheep in this apartment.... Nothing more was said about the possible sacrifice except that the sheep would be a matter of Islamic charity—and that it also would have something to do with the new red Toyota.

Sunday morning arrived with a deep gray sky and dreary light rain, but we set out in the little red car to find a sheep. There were four of us: Ismet, his father— the patriarch of the clan—Ismet's five-year-old son, and myself. Sacrifice seemed to be a male business. Soon we arrived at the foot of a hillside in a poor section of central Ankara, and were walking up a muddy slope scattered with sheep pens. The owners stood about in the soft rain, alert, prepared to bargain. The stoic and rain-bedraggled sheep were prepared to die, although they did not know it. Ismet's father was the authority here; after examining several sheep, testing their flesh with probing hands, he selected one—bargained—and the sheep was paid for (c $60), bound by the legs, and put in the trunk of the new Toyota. (I was standing about, fascinated, with no idea what would come next.)

We drove perhaps a half mile and soon parked beside a very ordinary concrete building. Ismet and his father entered, and soon returned with an Islamic butcher who carried the sheep inside. We all followed, entering a medium-sized room with one marble wall topped by an Arabic inscription from the Koran. At the foot of the wall, a small gutter ran along the floor. And here the sheep, passive and quiet, was laid down by the wall.

We were in an Islamic charity kitchen. Later Ismet told me that in the brief conversation that followed in Turkish, the butcher formally agreed to sacrifice this sheep for the Cok family, in the name of Allah. In the name of Islamic charity. Then, butcher and sheep were facing the marble wall; the man's knee pinned it down, his left hand held its muzzle—and in his right hand now there was a heavy knife.

Suddenly the butcher was praying—a harsh, enormous voice flung against the marble wall and rebounding fiercely in the now-small room. The prayer was hard as hurled stones, words fierce with purpose, words like sharp pebbles against a face. But the words spoke of Charity, obligations of Kindness, the Duty of man to his fellows. **We must take care of each other**. The knife moved quickly, briefly. The sheep moved once, once again, then not at all. The throat was cut, the blood ran down the marble trench. The butcher's body had shielded the knife from the child, but the child understood and accepted. The sheep was now the food of the poor of Ankara.

This charity kitchen was the property of the Municipality, and operated by Islam, by Islamic rules. While the sheep was being butchered—in 15 minutes it was skin and meat and bones—I was shown through the kitchen operation. It fed 240 men hot meals twice a day, and had a ton of donated meat in reserve in its freezer locker. I was shown a kitchen where smiling women were preparing and stirring large cauldrons of soup, and then introduced to the manager. All of them seem happy, gratified that a foreigner had come and seen their work. And I sensed, correctly I hope, a main point: the act of charity was personal and direct. The sheep had been delivered personally to those who need. One of Islam's "five pillars," its core teachings, involves the obligation to commit charitable acts.

Two thoughts follow me whenever I remember the charity kitchens of Islam. One is that in Turkey essentially no one goes hungry; the Turks have a saying: *if one man eats and one watches, trouble follows.* The other thought is a quote attributed to Gandhi: *To the millions... who go without two meals a day, the only acceptable form in which God dare appear is food.* In my own country, the richest on earth, people go hungry.

One last aspect of this story apparently has nothing to do with Islam. It has to do with Mal Occhio, the Evil Eye. The moment the sheep was dead, Ismet borrowed the bloody knife from the butcher and we all went outside to the Toyota Corolla. Under the patriarch's guidance, Ismet carefully dabbed three spots of blood on the tread, sidewall, and metal rim of the right rear wheel. Then the same for the right front wheel. After a quick return for more blood from the motionless sheep, the left wheels were decorated with the same triad of blood-spots, and the little red car was now, *Inshallah*, safe from traffic accidents, safe from the eye of ill fortune. *Inshallah*, God willing. Somewhere along the line Ismet had acquired a little smear of blood on the middle of his own forehead. He later took a small vial of blood home and dabbed a spot on Figan's forehead. My modern and progressive hostess happily accepted it. A visiting intellectual friend showed contempt for this pagan Anatolian practice, and my reflex response was to request a spot for my own forehead. If one has once seen Ankara traffic, one realizes that it is wise to take every possible precaution. For both car and man. A few days later, Ismet remarked, "I sacrificed a sheep for my car."

All the modern religions are, after all, accompanied by pagan elements. Paraphrasing Wm. Buckley, *The great flaw of the intellect lies, surely, in the planted axiom that what a man cannot explain he ought not to engage in.* What a poor place the world would be without magic! I once rode on a hideously narrow, curving mountain road in Greece in a bus with four bald tires. In the front of the bus hung a crucifix, a horse-shoe, a glass eye to ward off the evil-eye, a garlic bulb—potent against the evil-eye and nearly 100% effective against vampires— and an icon in a shelter lit by a tiny light bulb. Don't mock all this! There are places on that road on Naxos where a blown tire would send that bus four hundred feet straight down to the sea. Didn't happen.

A bit more than a month after my wonderfully warm-hearted visit with the Cok family, I was in

Bodrum for the Turks' most important religious and secular holiday of the entire year—the Sacrifice Festival, or Bayram. For many secular Turks this may be less a Muslim pilgrimage than the chance for a glorious four or seven day family holiday. As I shall describe fully on another occasion, the streets of Bodrum were virtually one huge sheep market. The sheep were dragged from the selling place on a rope by children, carried in the trunks of taxis, and on the shoulders of men, and trundled off in wheelbarrows. On Bayram Sunday—re-enacting Abraham's sacrifice of a ram in substitution for his son Isaac—after the morning prayers, all over Bodrum the head of each household cut the throat of a sheep. Or a goat, if he were a poor man. Or if he had no stomach for doing his own work in the back yard or the court, he took his animal to the Islamic butcher. Thousands of sheep hung and dripped blood from the back yard porches and trees of Bodrum. In Turkey, perhaps two and a half million sheep were sacrificed, along with no small number of goats. The rich sacrificed a bull, the very poor would manage a rooster. But all over Turkey several days of feasting climaxed on Sunday in a glorious day of eating and drinking, and the Islamic kitchens were piled high with the meat of charity. Often the skins also went to charity. In the entire world of Islam, possibly 80 million sheep were ritually sacrificed in memory of Abraham's near-sacrifice of Isaac.

We all have our own rituals and peculiar customs; many Christians, for example, go about ritually drinking the blood and eating the flesh of Christ! Kipling once remarked something to the effect that, "there are facts to be explained when you have time.

Meanwhile, you can laugh at them." A nice comment. In 1996, Brigitte Bardot launched a violent attack on Muslins in France, denouncing the "horror of ritual slaughter" of sheep that marks Muslim feasts. In an opinion column in the conservative daily *Le Figaro*, Bardot, 61, wrote :

> "My country, France, my fatherland, has been invaded again, with the blessing of successive governments, by a foreign over-population, notably Muslim, to which we pay allegiance."

She said she might emigrate. An anti-racist organization in France denounced these remarks as repugnant, nauseous and unacceptable. There was a general outcry of reaction to Bardot's rather nasty remarks, after which she announced (*Newsweek*, 6/3/96) that:

> "If tomorrow Muslims stop slitting sheep's throats, I will find them the most wonderful people in the world. *I am not a racist if one behaves normally!*" [Italics mine]

Now, I am told by my friends that I occasionally belabor the obvious. Nevertheless, I am fascinated by this remark, and will repeat it: *"I am not a racist if one behaves normally."* No end of wonders may exit from the human mouth if the brain is dead or the heart has turned to windblown dust.

THE GOOD WHORE OF PALERMO

A reader's eye is often captured by a title such as this. I have known otherwise respectable middle-aged women who, visiting a bookstore, would abruptly stop in their tracks to peruse a book with a title such as "The Brothels of Bangkok." And therefore you are forewarned: this is a dull story. It is a story, in fact, in which nothing bad happens at all. Of badness there is only a faint whiff on the evening breeze.

Not far from La Vucciria Market in Palermo there is a large Piazza that consists entirely of a rectangle of concrete surrounded by a number of banks and a rooftop machine gun nest. This is a banking square, and this is a Mafia neighborhood. During daylight hours on weekdays, the Piazza is covered with parked automobiles, pedestrians, perhaps 20 policemen, and a soldier in a sentry box carrying an automatic weapon. Of all this, at night only the solitary sentry remains; most of the good citizens of Palermo have locked themselves into their houses. My hotel overlooked this square. The man at the hotel desk was a rigid and frightened old Cattolico with the eyes of a hanging judge, and a bitter steel-trap mouth. His mouth said, "Be back to the hotel by midnight. Then we lock the door." His eyes said, *Don't go out after dark at all.* At night the Piazza was a place for whores.

One rather subdued young woman was a regular fixture at the corner just opposite my third floor window, but six or seven others often came by and idled there. Often these girls laughed and joked with the carloads of young men who drove by to look them over. Often a car would circle the block, and the men would laugh and wave as they slowly drove by again. The girls would wave, and kick out their beautiful, long legs. The car would circle the block again, perhaps, and one of the girls would briefly pop up her blouse, with a peal of laughter, to expose her ample breasts. The banter was generally around issues of the flesh and about manhood. "You boys are just making noise, you are children. You can't afford us. And if you had the lira, you wouldn't know what to do, Si? We would have to teach you, Si? So boring." And then, an old, tiny red Fiat stopped to chat—and the engine died. The Fiat would not go....

When the Fiat died, two girls happened to be at the corner. Instantly, the two jumped behind the Fiat and pushed furiously; the little car rolled away briskly, the engine caught and roared, and the little red Fiat disappeared around a corner and out of sight. To me, this seemed a bit odd. Surely the Fiat carried potential customers, who else would be abroad in the Mafia precincts of Palermo after nightfall? The girls were helping their customers to leave? But wait! Here came the little red Fiat around the block and up to the curb again. And again, when it stopped the engine died. One of the two girls had left. The other immediately stepped again behind the little car and, her long bare legs working furiously, pushed it slowly ten feet or so. Where it rolled to a stop, going nowhere. Just then a motor scooter roared around the corner. With an air of complete confidence, the young prostitute stepped into the street. Planting her legs well apart, she held up an imperious, high right arm and hand. STOP, said her body; she was as confident as any policeman in Sicily, and the men screeched to a halt. She pointed at the Fiat, commanded the two young men, and they leaped behind the car; instantly it rolled busily away, the engine caught and roared. Fiat was away and gone. And around the block, back, and stopped again at the curb! This last time the driver managed to keep the motor going, and a good humored conversation continued for fifteen minutes or more. Eventually, perhaps certain commercial arrangements were made....

Now, surely I am not such a romantic that I will offer up the regular girl on this corner as the "good whore" of Palermo simply because she has a good heart when faced with a stalled car. No. Whoring is not, after all, a satisfactory living except for the poor of body or soul, and the good-hearted whore is generally a creation of the film industry. Also, at first glance perhaps only God can truly identify a good heart. Later on that particular evening, however, God happened to pass through the Piazza in the person of a heavy old mother leading two little children by either hand. I had the impression, at first, that she was going to ignore the younger woman and simply pass by. But then she slowed, and gradually came to a halt. She turned, paused, looked. The old mother looked at the whore, walked slowly up to her, and they talked quietly for a few minutes while the two children stood by her side. Then the mother quietly said her goodbye, preparing to walk on with the children, and at that moment she gave her own judgment. With the children still at her side, holding her two hands, the old woman leaned up and gently kissed the whore on one cheek. Then she kissed her on the other cheek. Then she slowly walked home with her two children to make the evening meal.

THE OWL AND THE PUSSYCAT

The Owl and Pussycat Bookshop is a tiny den of musty old books in a lovely small city on a narrow peninsula on the Mediterranean shore. The shop has rock walls and a flat roof, a worn brick floor, a few benches and chairs and two little tables. The inside is post and beam, and two of the posts sit on ancient Roman marble capitols. The shelves are rough boards. The town is four thousand years old. It has Roman gates and walls, a Crusader castle on the end of the peninsula, and a beautiful, sheltered little harbor. It lies on the ancient coastal trade route between Tyre and Marseille, which of course covers most of the Mediterranean. I regret that I cannot be more exact, and name the town, but I would like to protect the Owl and the Pussycat. They may need a little protection—for Owl and Pussycat is a bookshop, but the Owl and the Pussycat are also of flesh and blood.

Bookstores on the Mediterranean shores are a very different proposition from those in the U.S. In my own country, the purpose generally is to buy and sell, generate financial gain and, secondarily, offer entertainment or knowledge. In essence a bookstore in the U.S. is no different from a store selling clothes or food. At the front counter is a computer, the computer makes receipts, and that is the point: receipts. In the Mediterranean, however, no sane man would attempt monetary gain from book selling; if his skills would keep a bookstore afloat, much less profitable, he would

make a fortune in ordinary commerce. The Mediterraneans are not, by and large, a people who read and
write. Certainly the men read newspapers, for political
news and football, but their lives are in the street and
marketplaces, and their great talent is in talk and
oratory. They are an outdoor, oral people. A believer
may refer often to the Book of his God and may call his
fellows the People of the Book, but he has seldom read
it, and seldom comprehends. [His priest or Imam
commonly needs to tell him its message when he visits
the House of God, and that man generally is no
scholar.] What then is a bookshop in the Mediterranean?
It is the stopping place of the traveler. It is the café of the
eccentric—and of the intellectual, who in the Mediterranean is the unhappiest of men. It is the den of the
unemployed University Professor, the failed priest, the
intelligent, the lonely, the ones who love talk, ideas,
music, the world of the soul. In short, the Mediterranean bookstore is not a place for the making of profit,
but for the dispensing of profit. It is the church of the
most sacred thing in the world, a book, and the refuge
of those who love ideas. The bookshop is the home of
the irrelevant and unemployed saint.

The Owl was a heavyset middle-aged man with a
powerful, rumbling voice that moved from thought to
thought, and from mood to mood, with the sudden
shifts of a damned soul wandering barefoot on the sheet-
metal roof of hell. He was a man of great intelligence
and vast range of thought. His idea of dialogue was to
ask "What is the last book you read?"— and then prime
the pump. The subject was not important: the political
science of Civilizations, the psychology of Aldous
Huxley, or Egyptian short fiction, anything would do.

And his voice resonated as a powerful, beautifully made organ in the company of a string quintet. The Owl had the appearance to play Oliver Cromwell, and the voice to fill a theater as Sir Thomas More. If he were not a depressed man, in the U.S. his voice would easily have carried him to elective office. The Owl lived a rather simple life, one suspects, and had many friends. They were, classically, the intellectual and the expatriate, the irrelevant and the half-sane. I never met a saint in the Owl and Pussycat, but a saint surely lived nearby .... Perhaps, for all I know, the Owl himself was a saint, but likely not.

The Pussycat was the least identifiable girl I ever met. I call her a girl. Pussycat was a woman of perhaps twenty-five, but she had "innocent young girl" stamped all over her. The only time I met her she was completely draped in a dark, voluminous dress and a dark robe, concealing her figure. These would have kept her warm in an icy climate, but this was a sunny and merely cool day; I assumed she was garbed to avoid male harassment. She quietly wandered into Owl and Pussycat and sat down on a low bench. Owl was talking with me when she came in, about a book, of course, and the Pussycat sat quietly and waited. She had black hair, pale skin, and was attractive in the way of a beautiful child who has not yet quite shed her baby fat. Pussycat listened to the Owl. She sat quietly, inert, in profile to me, and as the Owl talked I watched her. She was, I suppose, pretty—but she did not make a strong impression. The Owl turned to her, introduced us; she spoke, and then the Pussycat made a very strong impression indeed. Her voice was remarkable, and did not fit her appearance in the slightest. The voice glowed with intelligence. It was cultivated, soft, engaged. It was Bach on a dark night, with rain dripping from the eaves of a forest cabin. The voice was every intelligent man's dream. It was also rather unusual. And what she said in the next few minutes made little sense. In fact, it was bizarre. It was lies.

The Pussycat's accent was quite unidentifiable to me, but vaguely European—and she had introduced herself as an American. She was not pleased when asked about her accent, and responded, "My parents were Russian." But she was pleased when I appeased her by saying, "It's more a style of speech than an accent." In a few minutes much was clear: the Pussycat's words were those of an American, she had lived there, but she was quite Russian and wanted to hide that. What was she doing in Turkey? "I live here now, and in a tiny village east of here. I work here, and live there, and go back and forth as I please. I am going to make enough money to buy land and build a wonderful stone house, in the old style, on a hill above the village. I will live there overlooking the sea." Nonsense, lies of omission, all of it, I thought. Neither Latin nor Greek, neither Turk nor Arab, will give a pretty Euro a job where she comes and goes as she pleases. Much less a job where she can gain any savings, much less the money to buy land and house overlooking the sea. On the backs of her often poor hosts on the Mediterranean shores? These residents have been at their trades for five thousand years, they are better businessmen than that! At any likely job, this innocent, sweet girl will get room, board and pregnant, nothing more. If she is lucky, a man will marry her and not beat her. What is going on here?!!

We talked enjoyably for a very few minutes, and made tentative plans to chat over a lunch the next day.

That lunch never materialized. Soon the Pussycat departed, leaving me greatly curious about the lies. My
general impression, however, was of a very bright
drifter—an aimless and fairly innocent young Russian-
American girl of educated family. The Mediterranean
shores are scattered with them, mostly Brits and North
European girls seeking warmer climates and hearts.
However, a few moments after Pussycat departed, the
Owl rumbled forth with one of the most obscene remarks man ever spoke of woman. Unrepeatable, savage, ugly, he spoke of the excessive size of a part of
female anatomy, and he spoke with hate. I would have
been less surprised if someone had dropped a board
on me from the roof of a building.

Pussycat had left the city for her village. Eaten alive
by curiosity, I thought of going after her—but the stu-
pidest sight in the world is a man pursuing a strange
woman cross-country. No. This I would not do. However, it developed that many people in the city knew
Pussycat and most spoke of her with affection. Soon
the reality became clear. The reasons are never clear,
but it soon became easy to construct an imaginary conversation. When she wished, the Pussycat was capable
of great honesty. This is what she would say, on the
testimony of her friends.

Where am I from? Moscow. But I was raised in
New York, my parents still live there. Both cities are
cesspools. A plague.

Why am I here? I was to be the "brilliant son" of
my University Professor parents. In Moscow they
worked very hard to afford a tiny flat and decent food.
In New York they do no better, and hate it. I should
follow in their steps? When I was eighteen and had a

scholarship to Columbia, I sold what little I had and came here. I ran away. One like me always survives. But I want much more than that. Much.

What do I do? Oh, that. If you wanted to spend five days with me—it would cost you $1000-$2000 American. In advance. And worth it. You want? Oh, can't afford! Well, New York taught me about proper prices. Pay or go without.

How such price? I have five regular clients here, some of the wealthiest men in the city. I am not a whore after all .... you do know the difference? A very large difference. I speak six languages fluently, I can pass everywhere. One of my clients takes me on trips all over the world and introduces me to famous men— as his daughter! That is fun. Sometimes in their eyes you can tell they don't know whether to believe!

What do I want? That question is beginning to re-peat itself, sir. I have told you. Obviously, much more than survival. Comfort. Wealth. Fun. You don't be-lieve me? What does *that* mean! Oh, all right—there is a man in my village, he is very, very beautiful. I love him. He makes no money. We will build the stone house and live together over the sea. Who could want more? You don't accept what I say! You want something else? *What?*

WHY? "WHY" do I do this? I am fed up with you. "Why" is the most useless question in the world. Does the murderer really know WHY he kills? Come on! I give you one last thing, and then we are done. I saw a scrap of something in an old New Yorker—I am from New York, after all. It was a few words only, a poem. *And remember, my life has been a plague.* Moscow, New York, *many things I do not tell you. My life has been a plague* .... The poem ... was about the plague. It went like this....

In the old times
when the plague came
people would cast off their
sense of self,
say what was on their minds,
find what had
always been in their minds
but had remained unsaid
even to themselves.
Then they say what is true.
Then they remember
they are going to die
and make love to strangers.

I make love to strangers.

SOMETHING FAKED, SOMETHING NEW, SOMETHING STOLEN, SOMETHING TRUE: THE ANTIQUITIES BAZAAR

The eastern end of the Mediterranean, the Levant, has been home to the most ancient civilizations on earth. Agriculture began here, the first cities, the earliest written languages, the earliest metal-working, commerce, the earliest recorded sophisticated thought. The God of the three great monotheistic religions came from the Levantine desert; indeed the subtitle of a recent biography of the historical Jesus referred to Him as a Mediterranean Jewish Peasant. One could easily say that antiquity itself began in the Levant. And for at least five thousand years, art lovers, historians, archaeologists and grave-robbers—*quite often the same folks*— have been collecting, stealing, forging and selling the relics of these civilizations. In the great cities of the Levant (as well as in London), in their bazaars, souks, and marketplaces one finds the "antiquities dealers," the antique markets, the old book shops, the "antiquarians," and also the thieves, smugglers, forgers, restoration experts, auction house agents and scholars who love old things. Or their profits. In Aleppo and Alexandria, in Beirut, Cairo and Damascus, and certainly in Istanbul and Jerusalem, in all these places and more, thrive those who love the ancient object or the modern profit. And all antiquities bazaars have shared certain attitudes for time immemorial: a selective disregard for the laws of man and God, and a love of beauty. Some, of course, love only the beauty of the ancient and well-turned bronze or marble or book, and others the beauty of ten-fold profit. Some of them truly love both. Some are very honest. Most are not, at least by the standards of Europe north of the Alps. Allow me to introduce you to a few of these folks.

Since many of them are my friends, and a few of them do not like me at all, I must be a little vague about names and places. This is a small souk, a bazaar, in, let us say, Lebanon—dealing, let us say, in antiquities, old books, documents and Arabic calligraphy. The cast is as follows:

'Rico—a talented salesman and producer of fakes
Onur—an honest man
Black Adam—a smuggler
Tomas—a bitter man
Abdullah—an honest shop owner
Leila—an ethical dealer and beautiful woman
Nick—a thief

When I first discovered the antiquities souk, I was greatly taken with the beauty of Arabic calligraphy. The small bazaar, perhaps thirty or forty tiny shops sur-rounded by walls more than a thousand years old, was selling a wide variety of antiquities and documents from the Levant, Turkey, Persia, Iraq, Egypt, and the Maghrib. Several languages were involved, but always Arabic calligraphy. I was shocked by the great beauty and also by the age claimed for some of the documents — four hundred, six hundred, eight hundred years— and I started buying. The stuff was my cocaine. I couldn't stop. I couldn't stop looking, couldn't stop buying. In the beginning I bought only for the beauty, and paid only what the beauty was worth to me. Single pages from an old Koran, often illuminated with gold and stunningly beautiful, seemed cheap at $20 or $50. I disregarded the claims of great age and assumed that they were all modern fakes; and indeed my first purchases were from a man whose main talents lay in brilliant salesmanship and in the creation of "centuries- old" calligraphy and miniatures. Rico sold me many beautiful old Koran pages and other documents. Some were his own work; others the work of hired talent. A year later, he confessed some of his more devious work to me, but in the meantime I had made a surprising discovery. Some of the Koran pages were indeed very old. If this is all fake, of no great age, then the Government has no interest. I can leave the country with my beautiful things. If it is more than a century old, however, I may be in legally and morally troubled waters. And in shop after shop I was instructed as to how my beautiful art could be smuggled out of the country. *In God's name, why should anyone care if I have bought modern copies? Perhaps some are real?* By the time my elementary education was over, I knew I possessed a few pieces of gloriously beautiful art that were four hundred to seven hundred years old. I learned a great deal about shades of ethical and spiritual self-deception, in myself and others. And I learned how to smuggle guns, gold, icons, documents, men or cocaine across international borders. Welcome to the real world.

"I bought a beautiful old revolver in Germany," explained Black Adam. "At the German airport, the x-ray machine operator saw it and protested. I said 'is legal to leave with it in a checked bag.' 'But you'll be caught at your destination,' said the operator. 'That my problem,' I replied. At arrival I picked up the checked bag, went into toilet, put gun inside my jacket, and passed out through customs. No chance they catch me. But if they did—with the gun was $5,000 in black money. Gold? I carry through customs before days of x-ray machines. Bars in bottom of an old bag full of dirty clothes, and I wear old work-clothes. I go to customs line that says 'Goods to Declare.' 'What do you have to declare?' said the man. 'Nothing,' I shrug. 'Why are you in this line?' 'Man at other line send me here.' 'Go there.' I go to other line, and play stupid; I am simple man and don't know language! Go back and forth. Soon they get impatient with poor, stupid, working man, wave me through. Never search bag of dirty clothes! Never. To send rare icon or small package of bronzes? Or rare Koran? My friend has a friend at DHL; another man has brother at Post Office. Take package there—the black money is under the package. For small things, $15, $30 ..... They seal package, customs not re-open. So easy."

At this point, clear that I was violating the letter if not the spirit of the law, I talked with the two highly ethical dealers in the bazaar. Onur and Leila had similar convictions. Neither would dismember an intact book to sell the separate pages. Neither would sell to foreigners or send out of the country any old material of museum quality, a significant national treasure. "How can you tell how old it is?" I asked. The responses: "Why should you ask such a question? It is my job to know. I am educated. Do not insult me. If I have a museum-quality Koran, for example, it would be worth at least $30,000. I *must* know—it is my business. First I call the Government. If they think it is important, they will buy. Or they may take description, so it can be traced if it shows up at a London auction. If they don't buy, I call private collectors who have much money and want to keep treasures in our country. If they don't want—then maybe I do sell to a foreigner. Or I keep." One highly ethical dealer confessed to me that he owned a treasure that he kept, apparently, for the simple love of it: an ancient Koran in early Kufic script and in perfect condition. It may have been eight hundred or nine hundred years old. And its worth? "Selling price? On a generous day, a quarter million; on an ordinary day, maybe $350,000. But I would not sell." And reverently he added, "*It is perfect...*"

In the souks, perhaps in any such place in the Middle-East, each of these people quickly becomes a distinct personality. Perhaps most share a love of both beauty and money, but there the similarities end. 'Rico, for example, is a talented calligrapher and a decent miniaturist, but he would not dream of developing his talent and giving birth to fine and legitimate art. He takes professional pride in his faking, and joy in his sense of superiority, when he sells a Jewish woman from New York City a pair of pages from a Jewish text four hundred years old. "I did the pages at home last night! Oh, I am very clever. And I make her very happy. She did not want new reproduction for $25. Oh she want old, old things. She go home to New York very happy and boast to friends about old documents at rare bargain of $100! Oh, she very happy when tell friends the stupid man in souk not know how valuable old things are. I make her happy—and I am happy!" (She will not have it appraised, *Enshallah*. God willing. If she does, she will not be happy, oh very not.) Rico sold me two pages from a 1788 book of Ottoman navigation maps. Beautiful. Very. Done on his kitchen table. I was not happy, oh very not.

Then there is Tomas, who is a very sad man. His shop contains some extremely beautiful and valuable antiquities and documents. He charges very high prices for them. He liked me a lot until he realized I would not pay his prices. Then he saw that I had become friendly with people he cannot stand. Tomas loves money. Tomas does not love people. His wife does not like him, nor do his daughters. Perhaps he has taught them to love money. Since women run the home in the Levant, Tomas sits bitterly in his shop. A smile fractures his face, painfully it seems, if a customer arrives with money and no sense. His is a life that bears bitter fruit. The taste of it is carved on his face, so sad. After he had been hostile to me for some time, I wandered into his shop one day just to see what would happen. To my utter surprise, he smiled wildly and threw his arms around me. Then he raced a few steps to a pile of books and raced back with a damaged 19th Century Koran in his hands. *"This is for you, you will like. It is very special. Very special! For you, only $1,000!"* At this point Tomas is smiling and gleeful. I, of course, was skeptical.

I examined this Koran carefully for many minutes, with growing incredulity. A complete Koran hand-done in Arabic calligraphy, and decorated in gold, cannot be faked as old. The economics are not there, it cannot be worth the huge labor and trouble. This book was water-damaged and the covers were off, but still it was gorgeous. Furthermore it was of a relatively rare "Rococco" style dating from the last century of the Ottoman Empire. I was completely bewildered. Intact, the Koran was worth *at least* five thousand; even damaged, two or three. *There are no bargains from Tomas.* I asked questions of other dealers. I came back again the next day and examined the Koran with great care. In the end I bought it, as an investment as well as for its great beauty. Two days later the truth crashed down. I showed one page from this beautiful but broken Koran to an ethical dealer, and....

"*It's wakif! We wouldn't buy it or sell it. Get it out of my shop.*" The dealer explained her reactions in terms of ethics and law and theology. *But her emotions? She acted as if the page were cursed.* The edge of the page held an Arabic word, a small purple wiggle from a pen or scribe. The word *Wakif* literally means "*pious institution.*" Its meaning on a document or a book: "*This is the property of a mosque, religious institution or religious governmental foundation and must stay here always.*" Its meaning in a secular bazaar was: *This is STOLEN GOODS.* Which is surely why Tomas offered a bargain. (The emir at my mosque has cleared me of responsibility.)

Onur is a quiet young man, dignified and intelligent beyond his years. "I could work in Big Souk, work on commission, make more money. I have enough on salary, and I like this shop. Happy here. We sell truly fine old things. Maybe I sell nothing for two, three weeks. Then I sell one thing for $5,000 or $10,000. I don't have to lie to people; we are an honorable business. If you buy here, you know you pay fair price, you are never cheated. Also I am a friend to everyone in Souk. Since we do not fake or lie, nobody needs to think badly of us. It is better...." Onur knows the magic word: Enough.

I have a warm place in my heart for Abdullah although I do not know him well. When another man in his shop was selling me a very old object that he claimed was from 1144, and briefly left the store, Abdullah said gently, "It's not really that old. Maybe more like 1545!" [Nothing like an approximate date.]

Leila is a beautiful young woman with a University degree in Art History and a considerable knowledge of antiquities. She is highly intelligent and industrious in the management of her father's shop, which has been in business for fifty years. (Outside the shop maybe she is a bit disorganized.) She is my friend; and has sold me perhaps the most beautiful book I shall ever own. Leila is on my mind at the moment because of a rather entertaining episode. Yesterday she arrived at the souk miserable because the water had failed at her home; her hair badly needed a shampoo—it was a bit of a mess. "Come," she said. "We will walk and I will find a beauty shop, get a shampoo. You can chaperone me." *ME? The first and most urgent duty of all Middle-Eastern men—far more urgent than, for example, gainful employment —is to keep foreign men like ME away from beautiful young women like HER! I am to chaperone HER?* Remarkable. Passing strange! Fun. Well, this is her city, but we walk all over town, visit a beautiful old, out-of-the-way mosque I would never have found myself—and no beauty shop. Desperate, she looks for a men's barber shop for a shampoo! She enters one, but instantly retreats in horror: "There are men in there!" They stared at her like stony little empty-eyed statues; she does not belong there. Finally we find a shop with no customers. The young barber, surprised but smiling broadly, gives Leila a luxurious shampoo. Smiling, lighting her cigarette, he jokes with her. His first female customer? During the entire fifteen minutes, while Leila blow-dries and combs her hair, the little boy who sweeps the floor stands five feet away and silently, blank-faced, thoughtfully stares at her. I think he has never seen a tall, smiling, pretty female with jeans in the shop. The surface of the world crumbles, nothing is certain any longer....

The last episode involved Leila and also Nick, a young Levantine who was a thief. I bought some lovely Syrian and Algerian calligraphy from him and took them to Leila hoping she would appraise them. Leila looked at them, and said, "These were stolen from our shop! Where on earth did you get them?" *Aiee!* Nick was a likeable young man. There was no evidence. In my country, under the Rule of Law, he was innocent. Somewhat to my horror I was present when they confronted him, and his face said he was not innocent. He was convicted in the court of public opinion, and does not work in the souk any more. Me, I just write what the world says to me. And in this case the world said to me, "You are a receiver of stolen goods." *Aiee!* I am glad Leila is my friend. I think it was Mark Twain who once said, "I've been learning all my life except when I was in school."

In the United States, it is usual that one man is my friend, and with another man I may do business. But it is difficult to mix business and pleasure. Since I have painted a picture of certain dubious virtues in the souks and bazaars, I should also emphasize that in the eastern Mediterranean warm friendship and generosity and kindness are commonly mixed with business. Not many years ago a shop in Istanbul might make an early morning sale, a second customer might enter, and this second man might be told, *"I have already made a sale this morning, but my next door neighbor has not. Why don't you go in his shop?"*

After I have done a little business in a shop, a warm friendship sometimes develops. After 'Rico and I became friends, he apparently balanced the scales against his earlier deceptions with bargains and gifts.

After Onur and I had done business, eventually we became friends. One morning he gave me a lovely piece of 16th Century Persian calligraphy. As a gift. And then he said to me with utter sincerity that in the future, "*We don't make profit selling to you. We are friends. We don't make money. We make friendship. Friend is more important than money.*" Onur said this to me more than once with heart-felt and earnest words. Now you, dear reader, may be a cynic; perhaps you see some of this as calculated. It is possible, with a sufficiently warped soul, to see the entire world through cynical lenses. But a dear friend of mine from Washington, D.C., once spent hours bargaining in a carpet shop over a small, lovely rug priced at $500. Merry talked it down to $200—and then finally decided she really couldn't afford it at all. She left for home without making any purchase from that shop. A few weeks later, it arrived in the mail as a gift. To this you have no explanation? It is simple, you are but a cynic. This is the East. Merry is young, blonde, beautiful, bursting with good feelings, and wonderfully charming. As the Arab Bedouin would say, "*Wherever she passes, she lends price to the sand.*"

ABDESSAMAD'S DAUGHTER

When my ferry docked in Tangier in 1998, I was approached by an intelligent middle-aged man who spoke excellent English. Aziz introduced himself as a licensed tourist guide, and showed me credentials. His price was $15/day; and all of this was exactly as a guidebook had described an arrival in Tangier. I said yes, at least for a day, since I needed to find a proper cheap hotel. He described three, I chose one, he took me there in a taxi—and the Continental was perfect. Aziz left, saying he'd return soon. About two hours later, as I gazed happily out of my hotel window overlooking the port, a man wearing a beautiful white gelaba walked by on the terrace below. The gelaba is the full-length robe worn by many Arab men and women and this one was a shimmering white-on-white material. I wanted one like it. A few minutes later I went down to the terrace to meet Aziz, only to find that the man in the white gelaba was his replacement. Abdessamad was an unlicensed guide, and I had been passed along into his hands; Aziz had more important fish to fry.

Abdessamad is a devout Muslim who prays five times a day. He is not an Arab, but a Berber from the Rif Mountains. When I met him, he was 66 years old and toothless; an intelligent, simple and dignified man who spoke seven languages. Born in the Rif, a child of "primitive" mountain warrior people, he had lived in Tangier most of his life. He had married, raised seven children and now had nine grandchildren. He said very clearly that his family was the only thing in the world that mattered at all. Although he could see Spain every day, and a married daughter lived in Gibraltar, he had never traveled the ten miles across to Europe. He said he could not bear to leave his family, even for 24 hours. To the tourist trade, Abdessamad is known as Charlie; some tourists apparently are not willing to learn his true name, which I believe hurts his feelings if he detects a lack of respect. Nevertheless, you can find Abdessamad by asking for Charlie at Café d' Paris in Tangier. He is an excellent guide. I told him what I wanted to see. He sometimes ignored me, and it developed that he knew better than I did. Apparently the guides of Tangier immediately and correctly typecast me when they found I knew of a Tangier celebrity, Paul Bowles. This truly wonderful writer and chronicler of the North African Arab/Berber world was 88 and at one point apparently near death in early 1998. [Several people that I encountered during a ten-day stay in Tangier wanted to take me to his door and introduce me. I absolutely did not want to intrude on the famous and ill old man; later it did occur to me that perhaps he would have welcomed an unknown visitor. I hope he was not that alone....]

Before I introduce you to Abdessamad's remarkable twenty year old daughter, Nora, you must know one last key piece of information about Abdessamad and his people. The Berbers have no written language; they are what we in the West would call *illiterate*. A better word-choice would be non-literate. As I have said, Abdessamad speaks seven languages well, including Berber, Arabic, French, and English. He may speak a smattering of several others, God knows how many. But Abdessamad is illiterate. When I asked him to write

his name on a piece of paper [I cannot remember anything unless it is written], he could not write his own
name for me. He showed me a card on which someone
else had written his name....

Soon after I first met Abdessamad, he urged me to
go with him on a one-day trip to the Atlantic Coast beach
town of Asilah, a few miles south of Tangier. The Thurs-
day Berber street market was coming up; we would
take a city bus to the south edge of Tangier, pick up a
bargain taxi, and go down the coast. I agreed. On the
following day he asked if his youngest daughter, Nora,
could go with us. A conservative Muslim, she rarely
had a chance to step outside of Tangier, and she spoke a
little English. Of course I said yes. We made the trip.
The huge outdoor Berber market covered the side of a
low hill on the outskirts of Asilah and simply blazed
with the myriad colors of Berber costumes and Arab
gelabas. Deep crimsons, intense yellows, purples and
greens were predominant. Piles of foodstuffs lay on
the ground or on low benches. Food sat in the afternoon October sunlight simply flaming with a dozen
shades of deep squash yellow, saffron, eggplant purple,
onion and tomato. Chickens were everywhere, submit-
ting to a wrung neck or being carried off alive by tall
dignified women in purple or crimson robes. Donkeys
waited patiently or staggered with heavy loads—often
a costumed old Berber woman sitting on top of a pile of
melons or citrus.

On that day Nora was impeccably dressed in a full
length pearl gray gelaba; the long pointed hood hung
far down her back. She wore tall-heeled black shoes.
Over her head and under her chin, covering every hair
and neatly tucked into the gelaba on front and sides,
she wore a soft light-cream head scarf. The lovely scarf

hung perfectly back and down over her pearly gelaba and on an edge one could make out in small neat letters, CHRISTIAN DIOR®. Nora was quiet, shy, immaculate, dignified, a study in contrasts with her surroundings. She was everything that a riotous, busy and colorful Berber market was not! Nora was a lady; the street market was an October harvest festival, it was Africa....

A few days later, shortly before my departure, Abdessamad invited me to his home for a dinner. He lived in a lower-middle class neighborhood where the people on the street looked reasonably happy and quite well fed; the women on the street were beautifully dressed. Happy kids everywhere. Abdessamad's three-room flat was small, simple and clean, the home to 6 or 8 of his family. Others lived a block away, but were there for the family gathering. The women were immaculately dressed in beautiful head-scarves and gelabas and were in the majority. The meal was superb: cold vegetables, bread, fried fish with lemon, and then a plate piled with superbly seasoned chicken, rice and olives. Abdessamad and I were served separately in the side room. Then we all watched football on the television: Morocco 2, Tunisia 0 at the half! This is important—Tunisia is a power in football! All of the family seemed pleased to have me share their dinner. Very warm-hearted, good people. Only Nora and Abdessamad spoke English, but some things can always be communicated. Nora was slender and very poised in a black gelaba, and seemed a bit more relaxed than she had been on the trip to Asilah. She was cautious and shy and a bit bird-like with me, but was solid and self-assured with her family. It is a beautiful family, and Abdessamad has spent his entire life and soul on them.

I have tried to give you a picture of Abdessamad and his family, yet this story—if it is the least bit special—is about Abdessamad's daughter. What is remarkable about this quiet, poised, very devout Muslim woman, barely more than a girl? Nora descends from the Berbers, a people that the French and the Arabs have often described with contempt. The Berbers were "primitive illiterate mountain and desert warriors. Illiterate bandits, uncivilized. Not only that but bad Muslims." [It took a long time for the Arabs to convert them, and they are not done.] So this was Abdessamad's world, these are his ancestors. And Nora? Let us ask her. I shall stop and let Nora tell you of herself.

I am an intelligent young woman. I am a good Muslim. My marriage will be arranged... but be assured I believe in the human heart. I have never been to Spain. Or Gibraltar, although one of my sisters lives there. I am quite literate in Arabic, French and English, and understand Spanish. My major at the University is in Philosophy... which includes both Islamic and European Philosophy and also Sociology and Psychology. I plan to obtain my Doctorate in Psychology and practice as a psychotherapist. Because I want to help other people. And, although I do not yet really trust this... in fact the whole world is open to me. Perhaps, who knows... perhaps some day I, the daughter of "illiterate mountain bandits, uncivilized primitives," perhaps I shall even visit Paris.... Yes. I shall.

Enshallah.
God willing.

NEVER LOVE A STRANGER

*T*he island of Naxos, in the Greek Cyclades, is a place rich in history and mythology. In antiquity it was named for Dionysos, the ancient god of grape and wine, and the celebration of life. In mythology Naxos was the place where Theseus abandoned Ariadne, and where Ariadne later married Dionysos. Naxos, in its associations, is an island of ecstasy and of abandonment. The following story may in fact have little to do with Naxos—perhaps it could have happened anywhere. This is the story of a storm, and a story of hubris, a story of pride. And of the Greek punishment of hubris. "For as I well knew," said Nikos Kazatzakis, "the gods are envious creatures, and it is *hubris* to be happy and to know that you are happy." Greece, in ways one cannot pretend to understand, has a sharp-edged way of shredding the agenda and expectations of the traveler. The world—this world—it says, is not as you think it is. You can *not* predict the future. You are not what you think you are. You are something else. And, traveler, your visit to this world will be determined by forces you cannot touch and cannot know, and perhaps by gods infinitely old. These Greek gods particularly, notoriously, do not care for exaggerated pride. Hubris.

Regina and I arrived on the same ferry from Athens one mid-October day, two solitary travelers, and stayed at the same hotel on the Naxos waterfront. A couple of nights later, I was eating alone at a taverna along the water when she walked by. I waved her in, and somewhat hesitantly she joined me. Regina was an attractive blond German woman of twenty-nine, tall and broad-shouldered, and splendidly built. We shared a dinner; she told me that her English was not good enough for easy talk, that she was not comfortable with it. But a half-hour into our dinner we fell into an intense political exchange and suddenly Regina was fluent. She was a mix of Communist/Anarchist/Green Party, claimed to be a West Berlin television journalist, spoke several languages, and had lived for several years in Greece. She had been taught in leftist circles that all Americans were Fascists. To my amusement, she was apparently bewildered by me; I did not fit the template. My lasting recollection of that first meal is that with Regina's shift into fluent English came a surge of animated beauty, sensitivity, and a considerable and wide-ranging intelligence. A delightful woman. To a solitary traveler, such a companion is as food to a starving man. We planned to share another dinner the following evening. It was all fine, and we were having a happy time. We planned to take the morning bus across the island to Apollonia on the next day. If that bus had gone, who knows what might have been.

My fate is to be slaughtered by my own imagination; the bus to Apollonia would not have changed things. In the middle of October's sun and sand and warm water, a first fall storm came—gentle, then violent. Rain, hail, wind. HOWLING. Sheets of water stood in the sky. Walls of water over the sea walls. COLD. No ferry moved. Nobody came, nobody went. After six dry months, the Greeks looked up in pleasure at the wet sky, and ate, drank, laughed, held their children, smiled. And endured the wind and cold. They waited. They don't ask for more than the gods give. The Greeks know about gods—they have been abused by more than a few. But now a screaming wall of icy wind and water raged over Naxos town. The tourists, in T-shirts and sandals, went about with pinched and self-pitying faces, slowly dying of cold and boredom before one's eyes. The tourists did not endure. They were wasted. At nine in the morning Regina and I walked to the waterfront. The bus to Apollonia is not— it would blow off a cliff. We stood in a moment of light rain on the Naxos waterfront. Regina was bored. What shall we do? I opened my mouth in a rare and dubious moment of spontaneity, and what fell out was,

"I would like to take you back to the hotel and make love to you." In the quiet drizzle of rain, after a pause, Regina said, "I can't say anything." Looking away ... "You thought that?" Pause "... Americans are so open." [A patent and ridiculous error.] But Arthur Koestler remarked in one of his short novels that everything has been determined in the first ten seconds; all you have to do is ask and find out what the decision was.

We spent the day walking, drinking, eating, walking in the rain. In the night we went back to the hotel. An incredible, beautiful, slow sweet night. Shyness. Smooth skin. Long body, the long body of a swimmer; love, smoking in bed, holding, sleep. Shouts, talking and laughing in German beside me. Much tenderness. What a lovely woman. What a lovely night. Dreaming. Sleep. We awoke early, in the wash of ocean noises, and as we warmed to one another—there was a monstrous concussion. A huge electrical storm rolled over Naxos town, simultaneous overwhelming strokes of lightning and thunder one after another. Some Wagnerian being was lifting the hotel and dropping it, battering it with a club. Not heard, felt. We were literally hammered by the blows. We stared at each other with wide eyes, and then burrowed deeply under the warm blankets. Soft, gentle, sweet, we hid from the storm and in one another. Lost from the world, enveloped in a shattering electrical cocoon, slowly we made love.

If this were a novel, we would hold one another while the world howled and splattered. We would drift the Naxos waterfront day after day in rain and wind. Ouzo, octopus, souvlaki, salad, wine, beer, gin, cappuccino, omelettes. We would listen to the music of Greece, Italy, Germany, Austria, the world. Touched, hugged, smiled upon by the love-filled world around us, we would love in the knowledge of love. Be happy, knowing that we were happy. Sin but know not sin, for this is a world where all things are possible and sin becomes no more than error. I told myself, God's Truth, it was all a make-believe. I must not believe this. And yet ... Perhaps, very late at night in the plash of rain and wind, in the tearing and the separation of the sea beyond our window, perhaps we would even talk of how it would be next year in the rain and wind outside the Berlin Opera House after *Don Giovanni*. If this were a novel....

Perhaps it was during that last night, as we hid from the storm and hid so deeply in one another... Perhaps— yes, I am remembering, it was then the mistake began. One of us said it: *"After the storm is over...."* and we spoke of the future. It all crashed down. If this were a novel, I would not have been so proud. For four days I had carefully reminded myself that this was theater, a wonderful "As If" with a girl half my age. But as we edged more deeply into one another, and into loving talk of the future, *After the storm is over ....* it all crashed down. At thoughts of the future, fear replaced all that had been. It ended ugly. Ended with cruelty and lies.

Next year in California.... No. That would never be. It was not a novel.

Reeling, still storm-bound on Naxos, I could not walk down the waterfront without running into Regina. In pain, I went looking for a place to bury myself for 24 hours—a thick junk paperback, something full of violence and stupidity. The waterfront bookstore had a shelf of English language junk novels. I pawed down the row of used books, scanning the thicker volumes. I did not look at the titles, they were irrelevant. I simply wanted a good read. Found one, a thick and worn used book. I turned it then, to look at the title on the spine, and winced in pain, remembering my pride in the past few days, my pride in this beautiful girl. And remembering the Greek punishment of hubris, I raised my face and my arm and shook one fist at the gods in the racing Naxos sky. Truly. I did that. I think I whispered, *What are you people doing to me*? The title of the book was *NEVER LOVE A STRANGER*.

AT TABLE WITH SEASIDE BEDOUINS:
A VISIT TO A MEDIEVAL KINGDOM

*M*arsa Matruh is a small desert city west of Alexandria lying on an absolutely spectacular stretch of Mediterranean coast. In summer it is the vacation home of upper class millions fleeing Alexandria and the sledge-hammer desert sun of Cairo. The rest of the year it is the home of perhaps a hundred thousand desert Arabs who live with their backs to the sea. In Greco-Roman times this was an important port, but most Arabs are not maritime people. The attraction of Matruh in Alexandria is for its wonderful beaches, but the town is Saudi Arabia. The women are not only covered, commonly in black, but many wear eye-veils. Even tiny girls sometimes wear covering dresses.

From the Alexandria highway just east of Matruh, small clusters of sand-colored one-story buildings are scattered across the flat or gently rolling rock-and-dirt desert. The surfaces of the ground are unrelievedly desolate: dry dirt and sand scattered with rocks and, near the highway, plastic debris. The colors in October are an infinite variety of browns, tans and grays, relieved only by the clothes on the women and the clothes-lines. In blazing contrast to the drear background, one may see intense scarlet, deep rich red, and occasional deep purple, or sparkling blues or yellows. To an ordinary Westerner this terrain is utterly desolate; at night, however, and during the brief winter rains, the desert is sometimes beautiful beyond description. And, after all, the God of the three great monotheistic religions came from this vast desert sky.

I was invited to dinner at the home of a man of Matruh named Hamid Massaoud. He was middle aged and unassuming in both appearance and manner. His brother, Nassif, who was with us most of the time, was equally unassuming but more striking in appearance; he often wore an immaculate, symmetrical white turban. Both men were intelligent, dignified, and kind beyond any possible imagining. I was told that Massaoud had two wives, ten sons and four daughters, all living in a large and well-to-do one-story home of twelve rooms. I was told that the two wives loved each other, which I have no reason to doubt in this context. From what I was told and saw, Massaoud is one of the patriarchs or leaders of an extended family of perhaps five hundred desert Arabs. It appeared that the family—tribe, extended family, or *Ashera* in Arabic— owned hundreds or thousands of acres of desert that would be worthless in the eyes of an American, for in a good year Matruh gets only eight inches of rain. *Enshallah.* But for various reasons it is not at all worthless land, partly because Matruh is now a boomtown for Alexandria and Cairo tourism. Many people grow rich here.

Massaoud is a wealthy and powerful man. He owns much desert land of agricultural value, a major gasoline station, and gas tankers that distribute to other stations; he contracts food and services to petroleum companies, and has a variety of other interests. And he is infinitely rich in human community. Who is Massaoud, who are these people? I was told that the people of Matruh, until recently, were either desert farmers or

Bedouin nomads. Now they are all, essentially, a settled people. But until recent years, well into the twentieth century I was told, "We followed the rains." There is no remark more evocative of the desert nomad.

I was taken to Massaoud's home in a widely spread cluster of perhaps twenty low buildings lying well off the Alexandria highway and perhaps two miles south of the sea. To repeat, the distant appearance was of completely desolate rock and dirt desert. However, ground had been harrowed and prepared; when the winter rains came, the land would be green with winter wheat. I was shown the animals. A wealth! Two cows and many goats and sheep, all of which supplied milk and cheese. There were chickens, turkeys and "doves," which we would call pigeons. The dove house was a tall dome of tan-colored cement. The walls incorporated hundreds of short lengths of clay pipe; some were open to the outside, for the birds to come and go; the majority opened only inward for the nests. The doves foraged for food, and the product was the squabs. The dove house, possibly fifteen feet in diameter and more than twice as tall, was a virtually cost-free meat factory! Massaoud's home was a quite large one-story rectangle with an interior courtyard, the home of at least sixteen people. I never saw the interior. Beside the main entrance was a medium sized, simple reception room; and here, with four other men including Massaoud and Nassif, I was fed a simple, abundant, delicious dinner of soups, salads, bread, meat and chicken. The previous day at a harbor café, I had been offered a choice of rice or macaroni, and I had said rice, but they had excellent macaroni. On this day, there were two huge bowls of rice. All of this was excellent in its seasonings. We ate sitting on mats at a low table that was simply carried in with food on it. Except for spoons for the soup and rice, we ate with our fingers. More pieces of lamb and chicken were repeatedly put on my plate. I must have more. No woman was present at any time. We were five men and two sons who served us.

These men knew absolutely nothing about me. Nothing. I was an American—from that rich and powerful place that influenced their lives, and sometimes helped their enemy, and sometimes opposed their beliefs. But they looked in my eyes and my heart and saw that I loved justice and kindness. Or they saw something, God knows. And they began to shower gifts on me, gifts I did not deserve and, in large part, could never accept. They wanted me to come live with them. They would give me—give—a comfortable house, which they described. They would give me the use of a good car, not like the battered derelict Toyota truck which was all they cared to bother with. All of my needs would be supplied, including—by logical extension—a servant or a wife. I am sure of my hearing in this matter. For the entire two days that I spent in Matruh, I was showered with gifts of food to eat and to take away with me. They spoke often of giving, and sending me, souvenirs of Egypt. What to send? Finally, after saying several times that I did not deserve such generosity—this was taken as a hilarious joke—I admitted that the one present I would greatly appreciate was a few pieces of the very colorful and beautiful women's clothes. Immediately, a lengthy conversation followed—of which nothing was translated at all, except for one fragment about perhaps a one hundred kilogram shipment. This is talk, this will never happen. But at the idea, I will admit to a disgraceful mix of feelings: mild horror, glee, confusion, delight at the fantasy of gifting two hundred and twenty pounds of gorgeous Egyptian clothes to the women of Corvallis, Oregon. Also, toward the end of the two hour meal I was asked, "Surely your daughter likes gold jewelry?" [All women love gold, that went without saying.] It was absolutely apparent that these men wanted me to stay with them. They wanted to know why I could not stay, and when I would return. They thought it laughable when I said I could not possibly repay their generosity.

The sun was low in the sky. I had been told I could photograph the children. I could not meet the two wives—"It is against the law," they said, the law of custom. But I could photograph the children. They gathered in the golden, dying light on the front porch. Some of the photos came out beautifully, and serve to remind me of this stark place and its warm people. Only one thing is missing: in these photos there are no females of any age whatsoever. Much later I asked why. *"The girls must learn the custom while they are little."* I saw no female in Massaoud's home; but as we left, two heavy women were walking between buildings perhaps two hundred and fifty feet away. Their purple robes and the large red containers balanced on their heads were simple and lovely in the last light of day. They had nothing to say.

In general, the Arab is not a culture that plants decorative trees or grass lawns. If he does, he is likely to be the oil-rich or the upper class under foreign influence. In elementary fairness it would seem unjust to ask a man to plant for luxury when he has no water and the surface of the ground in the mid-day summer sun would fry an egg in moments or kill a man in an hour. The Matruh people do manage to grow winter wheat and somehow irrigate a modest number of vegetables, figs and olives from wells. From the porch of Massaoud's home, stretching as far as the eye can see, the October landscape is scattered rock, dry dirt, and more rock. A Black American once said that it is plain mean to ask a man to pull himself up by his bootstraps if he has no boots. The same applies to growing grass without water. This said, it is also true that an Arab, asked to plant grass, would be likely to reply, "If Allah wanted this, he would give us rain. Rain will come in winter for the wheat, *enshallah.*" I told Massaoud that where I lived in the United States we sometimes received from Allah nearly two meters of rain in a winter, and to this he did not reply. Dead silence. It is difficult, perhaps, to respond to the unimaginable. I have difficulty with two meters myself.

The standard Arab version of paradise includes abundant water and green things. Visiting Corvallis, Oregon, for the first time, Arabs speak often of the green; and I have heard an Arab friend mutter *"paradise"* when taken for a first country drive through the rain. And covering an entire wall of Massaoud's office in Matruh, wall to ceiling, is a blown-up photo of a green, formal English garden. Behind the garden is a tall green hedge, and beyond that hedge is a green and perfect English forest. There is no other decoration in his office.

I promised Massaoud I would return, and when possible I shall happily do so. But when I think back to my hours at his Bedouin table, or look into the future, I cannot help but recall the Bedouin customs regarding the treatment of a stranger/guest. Saint Exupery, in his wonderful *Wind, Sand and Stars,* described a moment when he was a guest in the tent of two Bedouin brothers. One was a friend, apparently, and he did the honors:

"My tent, my camels, my wives, my slaves are yours."

In the Bedouin tradition, as I recall, a stranger who appears out of the desert must be offered three days of unquestioned hospitality. I was offered an automobile, rather than a camel, but the basics were all there. However, if the stranger is still there on the fourth day, he may be questioned; *and if he belongs to an enemy tribe, he may properly be shot.* In Saint Exupery, the second brother in that tent was hostile, and wanted Saint Exupery to know that he would shoot him if they met outside the protection of the French fort. Why?

"... you have airplanes and the wireless; you have Bonnafous [a famous French commander in the desert wars]; *but you have not the Truth."* It is possible that the men of Matruh looked into my heart, and saw Allah in my heart. However, the men of Matruh might have been quite disturbed if they had looked into my mind. And if they had been able to examine my history! I do not *think* they would have shot me, but they would have known quite clearly that I do not possess the Truth. Or a different Truth, which to them is, sadly, no truth at all.

THE HORSE BARN

She was an old woman when she told this story, and as bitter as the small, bitter olives that fall from trees on parched and sterile soil.

It was ten years ago. I don't think about it any more, not very often; my anger is grown cold. So I will try to tell you, very simply, without the anger. Just what happened. Ten years ago my husband of many years abandoned me, his wife, in front of the whole village. Because he fell in love with an English woman. We lived on an island in the northern Aegean, I don't tell you the name. But —*Malaka !*— I am a Greek woman, I am growing old, what does it mean my husband "falls in love?" I don't even know. He had his duty to me, his honor.... But I tell you now, what I did. You will like the story.

We had a beautiful house at the harbor. We also had a fine farm a kilometer outside the village. The farmhouse was large and solid with wood, and there was a barn for the sheep, one for all the tools, one for the pigs. And a barn for the five beautiful horses. Wooden barns, because we were rich. My husband—I don't even speak his name—loved the horses. More than me, of course.

The English woman came, a tourist with her ten-year-old son. She stayed. He couldn't take his mind off her. Three weeks later, "I am leaving, you have the house here in village, here is paper for owning the house, I am leaving." And—in front of the entire village!—he

put the English and her son on the farm and went on
with his life. In front of the entire village! He was a
rich, important man in the village. The village was so
surprised; people didn't know what to do. So for awhile
they did nothing. While my *idios*, my idiot husband,
went about with the English as if she were now a wife!
Unspeakable!

I knew what to do; I went home to my family in
Sfakia, on Crete. I forgot to tell you, I was from Crete.
A man should never abandon a wife from Crete. And
not one from Sfakia; it is the birthplace of great fight-
ers, famous Generals, and madwomen. And there I had
brothers, and my mother. My brothers were most especially interested in my story, yes they were. And we
sat down, my family, to decide what we should do.

What we decided to do, after a long night of family
talk, and ouzo, and meze, was something any one of us
could easily do. But two of my brothers both wanted
very much to go. Me also. So we all went. First on the
ferry, and then with a caique borrowed from a friend
on Samos who owed a favor. We went ashore on my
husband's island just after dark, and walked in moonlight a few kilometers on the goat paths until we were
on the hill above the farm. Then we waited. My brothers had brought a small bottle of terribly strong raki.
They sipped a little and we told old stories, very quietly, until the time of night when sleep is deepest. Then
we went down to the farm with the gasoline.

All the buildings were terribly dry after the long
hot summer; we didn't really even need the gasoline.
The buildings exploded in seconds. We made sure to
fire the main house so that the three could not escape.
We never saw them. Days later we heard they had been
at a friend's house for the night; they had not died. I

was glad the little boy had not died. The others, now I don't care. We heard that the police did not come for three days. Finally they came, and looked, and shrugged their shoulders. "Things burn down," they said, and went away. I know this because I have a good friend in the police. A man from Crete.... but I realize that I digress; this is not about the *idios* husband, or the English. It is about the horse barn.

The pig barn and the sheep barn burned quickly; soon they were nothing but piles of glowing, hot little embers, little red eyes in the night. And piles of burning meat. But the horse barn! I had not wanted to hear the people screaming in the fire, so I went and hid beyond the horse barn. It was the worst mistake of my life. I had thought I would dream later if I heard the people burn in the fire. But the horse is a big animal; it takes a long time to die, it screams as soon as the smoke begins, a monstrous noise, ten times worse than a man. The five horses took forever to die, screaming like demons, and went on screaming after they were dead. I hear them every night.

I ran to let them out, I tried; before God I did my best. I clawed at the doors, the screams in my ears like the fangs of a savage beast. I clawed at them, the doors already burning, flames all around me, and then my feet went out from me, I was in air, and then brief pain as my elbow cracked, pain as my rear hit the ground, pain as my back hit, then my head. I was knocked out. Then I was in water! I couldn't breathe; a man had me by the shoulders and my head was in—the horse trough!?? And one of my brothers, Yiorgos, was shouting, and the horses were screaming, and flames were everywhere.

And Yiorgos was shouting—"*Maria, your hair was on fire, it's gone, you look—are you alright, are you alright? You look awful.*"

I didn't feel the pain yet. "Yes, I am alright," I said. But I am not alright, I never was alright, I never will be alright. It's the horses. I feel so awful. This is much worse than just to kill a husband.... I guess I'll hear them all my life.

MY FIRST NIGHT IN A BROTHEL

What is the price of experience?
Do men buy it for a song?
Or wisdom for a dance in the street?
No, it is bought with the price
Of all that a man hath,
his house, his wife, his children.
                        —Blake

Once upon a time in Antalya, after the collapse of the Soviet Union, the Russian girls began to flood in. [To the Turks most Slavs are "Russian"— and in the Mediterranean, bad women are "girls."] The girls came on tourist visas and needed a renewal every three months. One particular Turkish police officer dealt with so many visa renewals that he decided to learn to speak some Russian phrases. His job would be easier. He found an English-Russian phrase book and began to write out, a few words at a time, the needed Russian. The essentials. One day he stepped out of his office for a few moments, and a European—on visa business of her own—was able to glance at the police officer's essential Russian phrases. The first four were—*and these are exact quotes—*

   —I'm sorry, I have to ask you to leave the country.
   —Your visa has expired. Now you must go.
   —If you do not leave, you will have to pay money.
   —Now, it's time to say good-bye. *God damn it, you're so beautiful!*

At eight o'clock tonight I am to be picked up and taken to the eastern edge of the city. I am supposed to meet three beautiful young Russian girls, and choose between them. *I am terrified. I am innocent.* Both. All I did was ask Ali what was possible, and he was a fountain of information. I have always avoided this business. The women are one matter, I love women, but the men who come and go ... terrible, some of them, monsters.

"Ali, do the girls speak English?"

"No, but you don't need to talk." [At this point Ali's face says I am a little dumb.]

"Sorry, Ali, I don't spend the night with a girl I can't talk to." Well... Ali will see what is possible. Later he reports that for ten million Turkish Lira everything is possible.

I badly need a drink. Did I say that already? It is late afternoon, and I am in an acute anxiety fit. Pure stage fright. I have been given the lead male role in the High School Play. All my friends will be there, right here inside my head. I have not yet met the Leading Lady. I have not yet memorized my lines. I HAVEN'T EVEN BEEN GIVEN MY LINES. This is what anxiety is. Between four and seven I down two gins and a bit of dinner. Then the arranger comes, an hour early. Probably a mercy. I make the taxi ride in a sort of passive trance. I am in shock. Surely this is a mild version of the shock-state of a man en route the gallows... who begins to *realize, finally,* that this may end badly.

The taxi pulls up at a shabby apartment building. I am *strangling* with fear of the unknown. What *am* I so afraid of? I *hate* being afraid. Of *anything.* Horrible feeling... And then my thoughts jump back. A few times in my life I have looked into human eyes—and nothing was there. A psychotic man three of us had restrained on a California street. A physically beautiful Russian woman selling junk in the Athens flea market. Bright blue eyes—like frozen blue marbles—and nobody was home. The world had become intolerable, the soul had departed, and nobody was there. Instead, in back of the eyes, nothing. Empty. Nothing left. NADA. I do not want to witness that ever again, *nothing is worth that*. I am cheated a million lira on the taxi. Par. We enter the apartment building, and I meet the Patron. Probably a Slav. A face of stone. I am told the three beautiful Russians are taken. *Not* par. Then, as I digest all this—still in shock from the sheer strangeness of it all— into the room dashes an apparition out of a movie.

Meryem is short and dark, with dyed hair, and she is Bulgarian. A young, slender little body; all flesh and bone, with no excess whatever. A red one-piece dress of some stretch-fabric, covering her body but not her legs. High heels. *All red dress and smiles, she is* out of a movie... The face is not really beautiful, in profile not even pretty. Her entrance into the room may well have a staged quality. Nonetheless she marches in with a face sparkling and shouting with vitality, humor, street-smarts, and brown eyes full of beauty and smiles. She marches in and introduces herself, smiling, asking questions. *In English.* The Patron, as I recall, shows all the animation of a well-fed turtle. The rules here are clear. I like? I pay. Now. His eyebrows ask. I answer with a nod. Happily. I *could* say no, no problem. *Sure* I could. I have been raised since infancy to say no to a Bulgar pixie with a grin like a sunrise—*Sure I could.* I pay the ten million and Meryem and I go for a walk. I am still in shock. The curtain has gone up on the opening scene of the High School Play, and I *still* have not been given my lines. I now begin to suspect what I needed to know: this is entirely impro. As we leave the office, Meryem asked, "How are you?" "A little nervous," I smile. "*No problem*," she grins. A *big* smile.

Meryem and I check into an undistinguished hotel a few blocks away, and a second-floor room overlooking a small pool. I have made love, but never naked of all illusion. No romance. No requirement to please. And perhaps, in an odd way, this alone makes Meryem worthwhile: no illusions whatever. What does one *do* without the narcotic, the fraud, of illusion? When faced with a lovely little twenty-two year old body with very smooth skin and a huge smile... and nothing else. Meryem is not really even a woman, although she claims a believable twenty-two. She is a lovely girl. [Hours later she initiated a grinning comic debate, insisting she was fifteen and *grown up*. And I insisting, No-o-o, fourteen and *not*.] Now she removes her clothes and smiles up at me, waiting. Waiting to be kissed... Whores do not kiss, but this girl is not a whore and she is waiting to be kissed... *Until this moment* I had been in shock, strangling with anxiety, but suddenly all that lifts and disappears. Standing there in her bare skin, Meryem holds up to me eyes full of friendliness, humor, aliveness, and a kind of awareness of my plight, and then there is no plight at all. I must have been afraid, all the while, that I would find myself defenseless and naked in a room with a woman—and nobody home behind the eyes. *Behind Meryem's eyes sits a nice person. It is that simple: Meryem is a nice person. From that moment, everything is fine.*

Later on I shall say more about prostitution in the Mediterranean countries. In Turkey, where narcotics are harshly punished but prostitution is legal, most of these women probably are much better off than their counterparts in the U.S. For now, let me simply tell about what I saw in a hotel in the beachfront suburb of Laura, in Antalya. Each room on the second floor seemed to be occupied by a couple. The girls often popped in and out of their rooms—friends chatting, laughing and hugging each other. The entire mood of the place seemed a bit like a girls' party. The girls—I am simply using the local language—all appeared perhaps eighteen to thirty years old. Attractive, apparently healthy, basically enjoying themselves. Most nights, but by no means all, are probably easy. [It is certain that on a bad night a client may turn ugly, and the night into a nightmare.] Meryem, God help me, wanted to go dancing. She wanted to go to the Disco! This is so far outside my normal habitat that—*No! Not!* So we went walking along the beach, and through the warm and dusty late night streets of Laura. We talked about the business, about many small things. We would like to have lunch and just lie on the beach some day, but the Patron probably would not approve. Small sadness in voice. The rules of employment....

The *Rough Guide To Turkey* contains an ugly condemnation of prostitution in Turkey. That passage contains errors, one of which is that you—someone— might help individual prostitutes to "escape." To the Brit who wrote this, I say: perhaps 40% of the residents of England would emigrate if they could. *Escape?* To where? Most, and perhaps all women in Turkish prostitution are there by choice, and *not* physical prisoners. The act is legal. To this Brit, whoever you are, I say this: your article suggests that women in Turkish brothels might be helped to "escape." *Would you please offer them good, gainful employment? No?* Then my own imagination can offer only two other possibilities. You may single out a woman and adopt her; or you may marry her. Meryem would howl with laughter if you offered to adopt her. And as to marriage? Well—I shall tell you a funny thing. Late that night, near midnight, Meryem and I sat by the swimming pool drinking (a beer, a gin) and nibbling peanuts. As human beings will do, you know? Every so often Meryem would shell two or three peanuts and put them in my mouth, touching my lips *en passant*. Nobody had done that for a long time.... And then Meryem pulled out her wallet and lovingly showed me photographs of her husband.

While you are considering carefully the complexities of the world, especially a world that includes poverty, I shall end by expressing a small personal lament. I wish I could find a wife or a companion who would sit by a swimming pool with me at midnight and put peanuts in my mouth. Touching my mouth *en passant*. The world tells me, over and over, that this I cannot have. *Why? Why?*

Then, just as I began to examine this exquisite self-pity, this stupid "Why? Why?"— I fell into a dream. It was another day, another night, and Meryem had long since gone away. I dreamt and then, eventually, someone turned on the diesel engine of a truck immediately below the bedroom window, feet away, and a hideous wall of sound crashed into the room. The roar grew to thunder, died away, and was followed— incongruously—by the crow of a rooster. Then by the murderous, savage noise of two dogs fighting over a bitch in heat. And finally, suddenly a great bellow from the loudspeakers of a mosque nearby in the darkness: the Morning Call to Prayer. Morning... Morning? The truck, the dogs and rooster, the mosque... the predawn sounds... at my Pension? *Pre-dawn?* I reached out my hand on the dark bed for Meryem. Meryem was not there. She was not there and here her story ends—and yet she is still kicking and thrashing about. Meryem wants a proper final line. Perhaps, as her story began with Blake, it should end with Blake.

Someone was shouting, "Why? Why?..." Again the storm of diesel explosions rose up from the street, and through the roar someone was shouting "Why? Why can't we move?" It was my beloved wife's voice. Snarling, "I can't stand that God-cursed truck one more night. Move! Another Pansiyon." I turned over, looking into the dear face. I thought of saying, Keep your shirt on. Then I thought that might be risky. So I agreed. We would move to a quieter place. She sighed and visibly relaxed back on the bed with a satisfied smile. For a moment. Then her face became very still and her eyes very large in the darkness, and she said, "I studied English literature. Very important! Do you know what William Blake said?"

"Good Lord. Blake said many things! How should I know what you are thinking?" But I knew what she was thinking, it was all over her face, and then she said, "Sooner murder an infant in its cradle than nurse unacted desires. Make love to me."

"What a nice idea! But are you sure you didn't add a few words of your own?"

"Yes I did. His last line didn't fit. Do you remember what it was?"

"I think so. But tell me...."

> *Sooner murder an infant in its cradle*
> *Than nurse unacted desires.*
> *Every harlot was a virgin once.*

WOMEN OF AMORGOS

Nineteen-year-old Lydia had never had a personal conversation with any of the young men on her remote island home. One day she and Jenny asked her parents if they could take a walk together for ten minutes. Looking at Jenny carefully, the father replied, "Of course, if you promise that neither of you will talk to any man during this walk." The speechless Jenny was twenty-two years old, a highly educated young Athenian who talked to whomever she pleased, walked where she wished, and would form a liaison if it suited her. She hopes for graduate studies in Theater at a major U.S. university. In other words she is a modern, simply here on the island for a vacation. These two young women, of similar age —and reared perhaps 140 miles apart — are separated by centuries. In the Cyclades, their worlds—their centuries—have rushed into collision on the one existing track.

In the past, most of the people of Amorgos were farmers and fishermen, and most of the women have always been chaperoned. By no means, however, have their lives been all of one piece. Only forty years ago most villagers on Amorgos lived simple, traditional lives, shared little or no cash economy, married, had children, spun and wove cloth from the hair of goats, grew old and died. Most people accept their world, but others are difficult. Decades ago a brilliant and hard woman of Amorgos left for Athens and the University, and is now an archaeologist known all over the world. Others left for Athens, became skilled businesswomen, and now have returned to own and operate small hotels on the island. On Amorgos most girls are rigidly watched. Some, however, wear the clothes of sophisticated Athens and freely associate with Greek young men; for them barriers to ordinary social contact apply only to foreigners. Occasionally an island girl cannot, will not, accept confinement; a few years ago "the most beautiful girl on Koufonissi simply disappeared in the middle of the night." The family was in agony, I am told, until the girl later returned with the husband of her own choosing. One must use great care if one wishes to stereotype the women of the islands.

The Ancient

At Katapola, the main harbor of Amorgos, a beautiful twenty-meter German racing yacht stood by the quay. In bright early sunlight five young men in elaborate foul-weather gear listened to a sixth as he sternly, systematically, reviewed their sailing plans and the readiness of their gear. So at attention they were, so military, the six might have been about some deadly business. However, the harbor and the nearby sea were calm and these men were not going to war, or to work. They were going to play. They simply had received a forecast of heavy winds later in the day.

As the Germans prepared for sea, an ancient Greek woman walked past along the harborfront. She glanced at them briefly; then the old soul saw me standing ahead of her along the water and she crossed herself several times. Curious about this ancient to whom I seemed a menace, I gazed at her as she passed. She wore a long, old, sacklike print dress of dull gold and brown, white kerchief, faded socks and shoes. And then I saw her hands. The arms hung down, and a life of toil had left the hands too large. Massive from use, almost club-like in bulk, the hands were rounded and the fingers partly closed. Frozen in the position of work. Frozen holding a tool. Any tool. The club-like fists will go to the grave frozen, holding a tool, a lifetime of tools, release impossible. Even the release of death. When the bones are dug up in three years for the bone house, the skeletal fists will still clench an imaginary hoe or knife. How could the mind that commanded these hands— how could that mind have grasped the German sailboat and its electronic miracles? Or the six young Germans happily going to play upon the sea?

Calliope

Calliope's face is nut-brown, with a magnificent smile full of vitality and satisfaction; several gold teeth shine in her large-featured face. I have never seen a finer appearance in an old woman. Her voice is very strong; she may be in her late fifties. Calliope and her husband live in a three- or four-room stone hut on a winter-savaged bedrock ridge overlooking the valley of Katapola, and keep about fifty goats. They live with a marvelous view out over the mountains and the surrounding sea, but with little protection from the elements. No one else lives nearby. There is no road, no electricity. Water comes from the sky and a nearby spring. In a recent improvement, a length of black plastic hose now runs from the spring. They have the goats, two donkeys with lush, winter-thickened fur, bread from the village, a summer vegetable patch below the spring, leftovers from Dimitri's fruit trees, the wind, the sea and the stars. One part of the family living comes when surplus kids are sold before Easter, but cheese is the main product.

The home has a stone-fenced dooryard, and in one corner a newborn kid huddles in sleep. The blue-painted door opens into a small, low-ceilinged room that is both sitting room and kitchen. It has one tiny window and the usual mementos and family photographs, many of the latter in ancient black and white. More than a dozen medium-sized wheels of cheese sit about the room. Two are the product of the morning, and whey is still straining through the tightly woven cheese-baskets. Others sit about in various stages of aging. Calliope sells most of them after two weeks and considers them ready to eat at a month. Aged for a year—one sits on a board suspended just below the ceiling—they become hard and strong and suitable, for example, in macaroni.

The old woman put bread and a plate of soft fresh cheese—product of the morning—on the table between Fernando and myself. The cheese was rich, vaguely sweet and, I realized with a mild shock, still warm from the making. Fernando and Calliope talked for a half hour or so. I left a small gift, and the three of us walked down the hill toward Katapola. Calliope was dressed in a white head-covering, faded old sweater, a print skirt, heavy tan stockings and shoes that looked suspiciously like fading old men's loafers. They could have offered little traction on the steep, eroded, crumbling hillside, but she carried a cheese in each hand and went down the slope on deliberate, sure feet. A short way down the trail, we were met by a young woman and two brightly dressed children. They greeted Calliope in the gay fashion of those out for a morning adventure, and they were carrying loaves of bread. Perhaps an exchange of bread for cheese was part of the morning agenda; Calliope talked with her visitors while we continued down to the town.

In my country, Calliope would be seen as living in bone-deep poverty. Stone hut, concrete floor, little heating, no electricity, no substantial running water, no road, car, telephone, no things. No THINGS. When she and her husband become weak with age they will leave, and no one will ever replace them on this place of ravenous winter winds. Her way of life is over, probably forever.

The Mediterranean hills have always teetered on the edge of poverty, and sent their children to the city or to sea. Calliope's children live in Athens. However, two things need to be said. For one thing, this Calliope— this old woman who milks goats and makes cheese— has a face glowing with dignity and apparent contentment. Never would I envy or romanticize her life, and I do *not* dream of an exchange. A creature of my own culture, when I visit this spot I dream of central heating, a satellite dish, modern medicine. But Calliope has had a good and satisfying life. And lastly, a purely personal note: Calliope is a far richer one than I. She has eight grandchildren.

Black Dimitri's Girl

This story is a fictional wedding of two unrelated citizens of Amorgos. Fiction, because I wish to return there in the future. However, both Black Dimitri and Daphne are real. Very much so.

Black Dimitri is perhaps the wealthiest man in Katapola. By reputation, he is a man who has never been bested in a business deal. I beat him. For this I can take pleasure, but no credit whatever. I ordered from Dimitri a half of a goat for a party at my hotel. "1500 drachma/kilo," said Dimitri; "it must not be only the front half," say I. Ten days later I went to pick up my meat, and he handed me the front half of a goat. When I refused it, a quite reluctant Black Dimitri split a new carcass down the middle and passed me one side. This I carried to the front of the large store, where I found Dimitri's 23-year-old daughter taking money at the cash register.

Daphne is somewhat homely, wonderfully intelligent, full of subtle humor, and speaks English very well. I had dealt with her in the past, and we liked each other. Her reputation on Amorgos is that of a docile and obedient daughter, but Daphne is past the usual age for a marriage to be arranged. It is possible she is not wanted? I dropped the goat on the counter, Daphne glanced at the carcass and said, "890 drachma per kilo," and punched the cash register. My brain reeled. Daphne knew what her father charged a foreigner for goat. She had last rung up an error in favor of a customer when she was fourteen, and was probably beaten for it. I looked into Daphne's eyes, which glittered. Glittered, saying, *I do what I want here. Didn't you know?*

Full of pleasure, but also puzzled, I sought out my dearest friend in Katapola. And asked, "It is not possible, is it, that Black Dimitri's girl would forget the price of her father's goat?" "No, of course not." Then he looked at my face, and asked, "Do you know the story of Dimitri's girl? She is a good and proper daughter, except she has not allowed her parents to arrange a husband. They have tried, several times. You see, she is the only child. She loves them—but they are very old. She waits until they die. Then she will be the wealthiest woman on Amorgos. Only then will she marry, to the man *she* chooses. In the meantime she is a good girl—and does as she pleases."

Jenny & Lydia

The two girls sat in a sunny café in Amorgos Chora playing backgammon. While the music of Mozart swirled through the bright air, they laughed happily over the dice and their coffee. Both were about twenty years of age, and both were the sort of spectacular island girls that seldom spoke English and were never allowed contact with a foreigner. One was a lush, sensual young woman who simply radiated the pleasure of being alive. Some time later the same two girls were playing in a field of white daisies outside the Chora. The taller pointed a camera while the other raced, one ballet leap after another, across the white meadow. She shouted as she ran, and the flowers waved in the breeze. "You like?" she shouted. "You like?"

A few mornings later in a café at the harbor, a loud voice from the next table interrupted my conversation. Turning in surprise, I looked into the intense, sensual brown face from the Chora café. "I said," she repeated in perfect English, "When you think of Greece, do you think of Melina Mercuri or of soccer?" She was playing with symbols—and Jenny was no island girl. That had been a large mistake. Jenny was an Athenian. She was introduced in the opening of this story. And a few days later on a Pireus-bound ferry, she described what it is like to stand with one foot in the Seventeenth Century, the other in the Twentieth:

"I was born in Athens, but I come often here to Amorgos. It is the best island. Why do I come here?

Amorgos is very beautiful, and I have no family here. Nobody knows me. I can do as I want. I don't like the conservative, macho, chaperone beliefs in the islands— but I do what I want. If the Greeks here see me with a Greek boy, they ask, 'Is he your husband? Are you going to get married? No? Then *why are you with him?'* Once I rode on the back of a boy's motorcycle; and to do that I must put my arms around his waist, yes. But then a man challenged us. 'What are you doing together?' And I went once briefly to a boy's hotel; that was challenged."

"The young Greek men are always watching young foreign men coming off the ferry and thinking, 'Is this the one that may take away the girl I could marry?' The island girls have more reason to worry. I was here for a week and an Amorgos boy asked me to marry him. 'And stay here; give up my career?' 'Yes, of course.' 'NO!' The boys worry about the girls, the girls about the boys, and the parents worry about *everything* foreign. The girls start marrying at fifteen on Amorgos, and are worried if they have not married by the age of twenty. Here the boys and girls can't talk to each other in any personal way before marriage. If a boy tries, the girl must turn away. Almost all marriages are arranged by the parents, and the girl generally is not consulted. She can say no, but usually does not; there would be consequences. Before marriage they know only the face of the other, not the heart."

"The girls of Amorgos generally want a decent husband and children, nothing more. I have met only one girl here who questions the system. She wants a voice in choosing her husband, but her goal is the same. Here are the biggest differences: on Amorgos the parents do the choosing and the dowry is routine. In Athens, not so. In Athens, the young marry for love— and there are many divorces. Marriage is arranged on Amorgos— and divorce is rare. If I am an Amorgos girl, sitting in a chair, and my father enters the room, he may tap me on the shoulder without speaking. I will then get up and give him my chair. Maybe I will remove his shoes. However, I am a woman of Athens. Perhaps I shall go to New York, Boston and San Francisco next year. Perhaps a man will give up his chair to me—but I shall not give up my chair to any man."

WE STOLE IT FAIR AND SQUARE
AND I THINK WE SHOULD KEEP IT

A few years ago the United States returned the Panama Canal Zone back to the people of Panama. During the U.S. Senate debate on the matter, Senator S. I. Hiakawa of California made the surely tongue-in-cheek remark that titles this essay. It is an uncommonly honest statement in the history of nations and it is also highly relevant to the history of art and archaeology. For five thousand years or more, emperors, archaeologists, grave-robbers, paid bedouin excavators, art collectors, sultans, tourists, university professors, and hungry men and women have been taking art and old things that didn't belong to them. Generally they didn't belong to anybody. Is it theft? If asked why they take things, these folks will give a thousand different reasons. Many of these reasons are simply rationalizations. I personally respect simple answers such as, "My family is hungry. I will take and sell this thing and feed my family." However, most of the explanations given by these people are less than completely honest; and therefore I honor the man who will say, "I stole it fair and square and I am going to keep it."

This line is honest. It is also the most humorous title I can imagine for a very un-funny set of questions. They are questions that quietly dog the footsteps—or *should* dog the footsteps—of archaeologists, tourists, museum keepers, art collectors and dealers, and the antiquities mafia through the last few centuries.

- I wonder who owns this stuff?
- Should I keep it?
- Should I buy it?
- How do I get it out of the country?
- Does the government really care?
- Is it really, after all, a treasure?
- And, if I am really justified in taking this 500 year old calligraphy out of Turkey, why do I feel guilty? After all, I bought it fair-and-square, and paid the black money to have it smuggled out. Why do I still feel guilty?

Forty years ago, when the world was young, a friend once told me that I had mastered the art of looking guilty while doing absolutely nothing. But that is another story. I have exposed my misdemeanors. Let us pass on to more entertaining and seriously felonious matters.

In the fields of archaeology and in the oft-connected activities of grave-robbing and art collecting, the following story is a prototype. The locale is Lebanon— or perhaps it is Jordan or Syria or Egypt. The archaeologist is British—or perhaps he is German or French or American. No, as I think of it, he could not possibly be American; he knows the Arab too well. The only certainty is that we are in Bedouin country, for we are looking at an archeological excavation through the eyes of an old, stout Bedouin woman. She is the dominant personality here, and she knows or guesses almost everything to be known. Everything you would never guess. The Bedouin women make excellent excavators, especially for the more delicate work. They have patience, they have skills. A few of their men must also be hired, for reasons of pride. They do no work. The excavation site was a Greek city of possibly 50,000

people well before the birth of Christ; it sits on a desert
plateau in Bedouin country, in a place that surely was
less desolate when the Greeks were here.

What questions could the old Bedouin woman answer if she would? These are some of them:

- *Which of the workers are honest?*
- *Which of them are Government spies?*
- *Which of them inform the Beirut antiqui-
ties mafia of new discoveries?*
*[It is not Beirut but it might as well be, so
we shall speak of Beirut.]*
- *Which worker would slip an ancient coin
into the front of her dress? Or tell of items
still in the ground?*
- *Which sells to the local, and which sells to
Beirut mafia?*
- *Which archaeologists work for foreign in-
telligence services?*
- *Which have been approached? [All of them,
most frequently by our dear CIA.]*

I have spoken of the old woman as the dominant
person here. Why? When she stands up from her work
and roars, *"It's too hot now (or too cold); let's go home,"* all
work stops dead for the day. It's the same old story of
weak, powerless Arab women.

What the Bedouin woman does not know, which is
little, the archaeologist does know. We shall call him
John, a name of many languages, and he is not only
quite intelligent but also unusual in his taste for life.
John is one of the rare educated Westerners who has a
taste for the bad part of town. Beirut is the bad part of
town. John has worked for quite a number of years at

the Greek archaeological site. When he learned of the Beirut antiquities mafia, he did what I would never dream of doing, not even in my wildest nightmare: *he went to their doors in Beirut, knocked, and introduced himself!* He did that. Probably he knew that the Arab respects courage; and surely he knew that the sole *raison d'etre* of Beirut is to buy, sell, barter, and deal. John spoke of such possibilities, and certain doors cautiously opened to him, and these things he learned:

The Beirut antiquities mafia buys and sells to the world. They know where their purchases come from and where they go. They would sell to London or New York or Tokyo, but also to him. And he found, through this mafia, a wealthy Beirut resident who possesses *"a private collection of antiquities that in its specializations is superior to any museum collection in the world."* [I cannot believe this; I just quote him.] John believes that the collector's motive is financial gain only—the collection is the main asset that will permit him to take his family out of the Middle-East before the newly rising storms of war. However, the collector *will not sell only a part of a horde of coins, or break a set of exquisite silver-working.* This fact strongly implies ethics or aesthetics that go beyond the usual Beirut souk. For his Government, John has bought—and is negotiating for—hordes of coins from archaeological sites in the region; intact, and with the site known, these still have great archaeological value. One last bit of information: this antiquities collector and dealer does not consider himself part of the antiquities mafia because he has paid for everything. "I bought it fair and square.... and am therefore an honest man."

When John recounted this story, I seriously doubted its veracity. How could the man and his collection, widely known, survive without a small army of relatives carrying automatic weapons? And, most emphatically, why on earth would such a collection be shown to a stranger who is a European archaeologist? *Come on.* In the ordinary reality of the day, these men are in mortal competition for the beautiful and ancient things in the ground. To meet in the marketplace and discuss an object? Yes. But for the collector to say, "Welcome to my home?" *Come on.* In the end, I asked John why he should be trusted by this man; his answer goes to the heart of the Middle-East, and surely is to be believed:

"My wife and children came to Beirut for a visit, and they got to know his wife and children. They all got along wonderfully; trust was established, and then all the doors were open. Once my family was in the city when I was not, and they were treated like visiting royalty. Better than I ever was!" Yes. With family, the man would be trusted.

Archaeologists and thieves are sometimes one and the same folks. I've never known an archaeologist who didn't have a few souvenirs at home. A University of California professor of my acquaintance, whose specialty was in Greek archaeology, had on his mantlepiece at home ten gorgeous Classical Greek vases. They had no museum collection numbers or identification on them, and sat there on the mantle waiting for the next major earthquake. Then they would be gone. We are all receivers of stolen goods; this is the history of Western Civilization. We stole it fair and square. No, I am not purveying guilt. That is not the point.

Many of the objects that fill the world's museums are indeed stolen goods—and the present owners are receivers of stolen goods—*but only under modern law*. When they were first taken or bought, no laws forbade such matters. A man found an object, sold it and fed his family. Or an archaeologist found it and took it to a museum. Irony of ironies, it is the archaeologist, art collector and historian who have taught the poor peasants of the world to dig in the ground in search of the old and the beautiful. Now we want them to stop! However, this is a cottage industry that goes back at least to the 3ʳᵈ millennium B.C. Objects were once robbed from a Pharaoh's tomb and turned up in another Pharaoh's tomb —twenty years later!

In modern Western Civilization, material objects are commonly possessions by law; ownership is defined by law. However, over most of history an object might belong to a man simply by right of possession. It is a relatively new idea that objects belong to a Nation State. Until the 20ᵗʰ century, the order of the day in most of the world was, *Mine by right of conquest*. Under either the British Empire or the Ottoman, for example, ownership by the King or the Sultan was by right of conquest. In much of the world the rules have now changed, but this is no simple matter. Quite the contrary. In the 19ᵗʰ century, a magnificent buried horde of gold objects was excavated at Troy by an amateur German archaeologist. His behavior was that of a thief. The Troy Gold objects were made by Greeks; the horde, technically the possession of the Ottoman Empire, was stolen by a German, placed in a German museum, and now—by right of conquest—is possessed by Russia. Several nations would like to claim proper ownership.

While in Istanbul, I have bought or been given an assortment of marvelously beautiful calligraphy. Technically, some of these may have been sent out of Turkey in violation of law. The Turkish Government knows that this art is being sold to foreigners in the Sahaflar Carsisi, and has no concern. On the contrary, the Government itself buys from the book market on the rare occasion that something of museum quality turns up. If I take what I have bought to an Istanbul museum, they will not want it. Nothing sold openly in the book bazaar is of museum quality, not even close. Nevertheless, as I have already indicated, the matter feels uncomfortable. My modest collection includes much Ottoman Turkish calligraphy, at least one piece of Selcuk (pre-Ottoman) Turkish from the 1300s, and a few pieces of Mamluk (Egyptian), maghrebi (Algerian region), Syrian and Persian. Probably most of this was once the property of Ottoman Sultans. However, let us close this story with an exquisitely beautiful 18th century Persian poem, a calligraphy that I purchased in Istanbul. It may have come to Ottoman Istanbul by right of conquest, spoils of Empire. It may have been purchased in Persia. It may have been done in Istanbul by a Persian. Or done by a Turk in Persian style. And although I trust the dealer who sold me this wonderful piece, she cannot really guarantee its source; it may have been done by a Turk a few days ago on his kitchen table. If I were stupid enough to be consumed by guilt, then—pray, tell me—to whom shall I return this Persian poem?!! There is no one. So I think I will keep it.

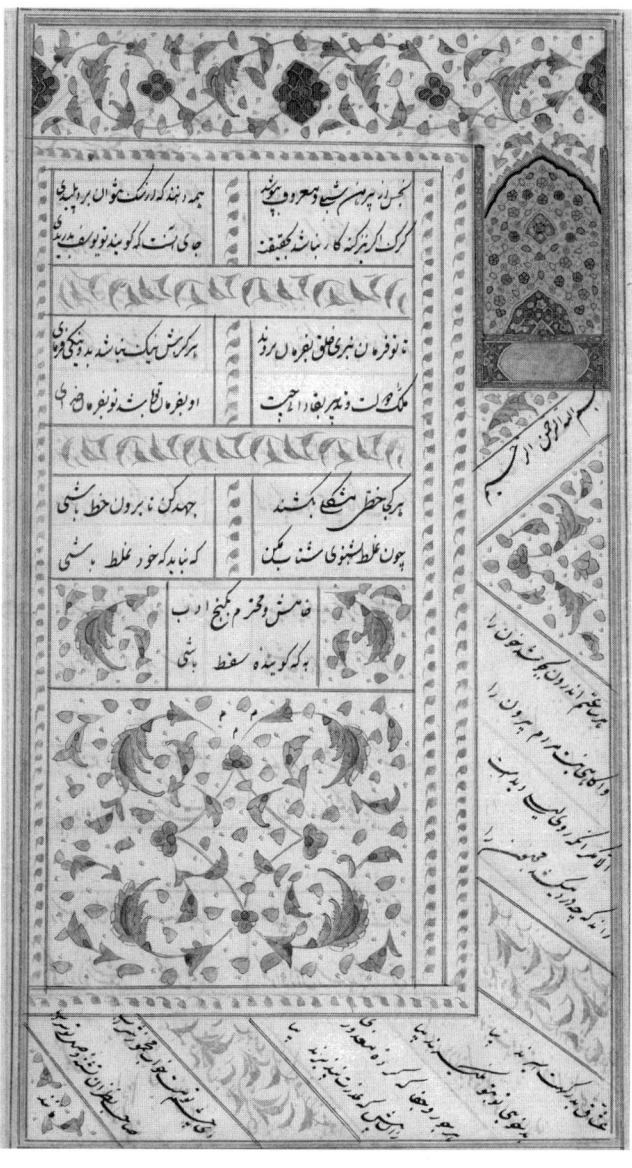

A GIRL NAMED 1003

She was a young girl in the nunnery at the Church of the Evangelistra, and her name was 1003. She had a name, of course—but when an English traveler named Theodore Bent visited the Greek island of Tinos many years ago, he knew her only as 1003. And when Bent later wrote of his travels, this is what he said of the nun who is known to English history only by a number.

"After our meal was over, a rather pretty sister was told off to conduct us round the place: we wandered into the houses, chatted with the nuns, saw their handiwork, and made some more purchases. Then our friend took us to the cemetery. What a horrible place that was! Just a small chapel surrounded by a few tombs, marked by nothing but sticks, with no other epitaph on than a number. The chapel was bare and unadorned inside, except for a terrifying wall painting ... and then our guide opened a door to the left, out of which a dank, fetid smell issued.

'Come in and see the charnel-house,' said she cheerily. As we entered by the dim light we saw rows of female skulls, which seemed to glare at us with indignation for disturbing their repose. To our left was hanging what looked in the uncertain light to be spiders' webs covered with dust. Our guide said:

'When a novice comes her hair is cut off and hung up here. Let me see,' she said, pausing and shaking a grimy tangled mass. 'This is mine, number 1003: when I die I shall be buried for three years, dug up again, my skull put up on that shelf, my bones packed in yonder cupboard, and I shall be entered in the dead-book as number 1003.' "

More than one person who knows the Greeks well, both Greek and not, has remarked that Greek attitudes toward life *and* toward death are rather pragmatic and fatalistic. Some would say pagan. Certainly the rural Greek's attitude toward death is different from ours, manifest in a thousand ways in every Greek country church, cemetery and bone-house. Death is not denied. Death is simply part of life. To me this might seem a desirable viewpoint to any person who hates a lie.

Be that as it may, I had a problem with Theodore Bent's story of the nun known simply as 1003. He told us nothing more of this soul; not her name, not her story. And so, she is known to history perhaps only as 1003. We, all of us, wonder how we will be remembered after we are gone.

> *"Say in your mouths the words that were our names/we will tell you all we have learned/we will tell you everything."*
> —Archibald MacLeish

To us her name is 1003... and somehow it felt wrong for that to be the end of it. I did not know why this young woman had been in the nunnery, or whether she had lived out her life there. I did not know her name.

She might have lived into my own lifetime, for Greek country women live a long time. I said to myself, after reading Bent's lines, that someday I would find out her name, hold her skull in my hands, and light a candle for her. I would tell her story. If I could not find it out? I would do my best. I promised myself, in the spirit of Herodotus, that the story would be either as it was—or as it should have been.

I never dreamed that I would actually find her—if alive, she would now be very ancient, and surely the Church was not going to give me any information about a nun. I did, however, have one possible entre to the records of the Church of the Evangelists; a friend in the Greek Diplomatic Service whose family in Athens had close ties to this church on Tinos. I spoke to him, he spoke with his family, and they spoke with the Fathers. As I expected, the Church was a stone wall. Even highly placed Greeks with connections to the Church of the Evangelistria were not going to get information about one of their nuns, living or dead. Normally that would have been the end of it—but no! My contacts had no access to the records; but just on a chance they bribed a Greek teenager on Tinos to make a 3:00 a.m. inspection of the bone house. Perhaps her skull was there, with 1003 across the frontals. A closure of sorts. *No!* The child found the charnel house door locked, for there were now foreign tourists on Tinos. He over-reached his orders, twisted open the lock, and— *the bone house contained neither skull nor bone-box **nor the hair** of the girl named 1003.*

Name of God, what did it mean? To my Greek friends the meaning seemed pretty clear; the girl had not remained a nun, or at least not a nun in this order. She had probably left the Church. Now my curiosity was truly aroused. After years of traveling about the Mediterranean, and speaking only English, I have mastered the art of smiling and looking pathetic. I went to Tinos, to the Church of the Evangelists, knocked on all the doors, asked the Fathers about 1003, smiled and looked pathetic. They slammed the doors in my face. Every day for nearly two weeks I knocked, and they slammed the doors. Once a Father did ask, "Why? Why do you want information?" Then he slammed the door. Let me tell you—looking honestly helpless will get you a long way in this world if you just master the act and repeat it. Finally an old priest said to me,

"You waste your time here. Ask at the harbor on Syros about the nun who left from Tinos. And if you are going to butt into our affairs, *at least learn Greek.*"

"*Thank you.* And, I am sorry but I can't learn Greek. I am very stupid with language, and I would also have to learn Italian, Croat, Turkish and Arabic."

"*Fool!* I should not have spoken to you! *TURKISH? Idios! Arabic?* Idios!" And he slammed the door loudly in my face. I should not have been quite so honest with him.

Syros and its large harbor city of Hermopoulos are a scant few miles across the sea from Tinos. On a clear night the glittering lights of either one are plainly visible from the other. But Tinos is a religious island, the Lourdes of modern Greece, while Syros was a typical Mediterranean port; that is, virtually anything could be bought or sold in Syros, and the rest could be made or bartered. I decided that if any information about 1003 was available on Syros, the quickest way to find it was to offer money. I made the rounds of the port cafés at Syros harbor. In each, I showed them a $50 bill and said,

"I want information about an old nun who left the Evangelistria. Very old. Probably dead. If you find her, or find about her for me, the bill is yours." The old men were interested.

"Maybe more than one that came from there. How we know if we find the one you want?"

"You find for me. I can tell from her, or the relatives, if it is the right person. Just find someone who knows of such a story. Then the bill is yours if it is the one I want." Finally an old man told me to come with him, led me to a tiny taverna back from the harborfront, and said to the proprietor,

"Alexandros. Your old grandmother? As a girl, she was in the nunnery at Evangelistria? The American," he gestured, "wants to ask about her." Alexandros was friendly, but brief. "My grandmother? What do you want? She speaks little English."

"Please show her this piece of paper."

"There is only a number on it."

"I know. Please show it to her and ask if she knows what it means."

He looked at me with much puzzlement. He left. And in a few moments, not more than two minutes, he came back. With great curiosity, and with a very firm voice, he said to me,

"*I showed my grandmother your piece of paper. She started crying. She is still crying. She doesn't look like she is going to stop for a while. She looks like a dam burst, all she said was, 'It was so long ago...' Nothing else. Who are you, what is this number, 1003? What do you want here?*"

It was she.

The day was late, I was numb with surprise at finding the old soul alive, and obviously was unhappy at reducing her to tears. I apologized to Alexandros for the sudden intrusion, asked him if I could return later, and beat a retreat. Why did I feel that it was a retreat? The girl called 1003—had a name! Alexandros told me! Her name was *Angela Mavros* ; the now ancient woman, once a nun and once known as 1003, was now Black Angela. *Black angel!*

By the next morning Angela and her grandson were recovered from the surprise, and the old but alert woman was extremely curious. Who was I? How? Why? All three of us probably were eaten alive by curiosity. I owed them an explanation, and laid out my obsession about a nun in an old book. A nun with no name, only a number. When I was done, and my story was brief, Angela looked at me thoughtfully and then made a speech. She spoke little English, Alexandros translated in fragments, and so the following conversation must be heard as a summary, a paraphrase of her story. As best I can recall, it was like this....

So you want to know my life. As simple as that? I suppose I am grateful to you. Here I am, at the very end of my life—and you remind me of who I was, and the foolish mistakes I made, seventy or eighty years ago. *Yes, more than seventy years....* It is an eternity. I was in the nunnery because I thought I had gone mad. It was my asylum. The nuns taught me I was sane, and then I went home. That is all there is to tell. The rest— I have been a Greek country woman.... and you have reminded me of a past so long ago that it was gone away. And now you come....

In the nineteenth century, Hermopoulos—this place —was a very important city. In the day of sailing ships it was one of the largest trading cities in the eastern Mediterranean. It was very European, very Italian. I was born here, raised here. My family was important. My childhood was ordinary. Hermopoulos has a beautiful opera house, designed after the famous La Scala Milano. We called it our little La Scala, and in the last century we actually had an Italian opera season! Now the opera house is long dead and decayed, there is talk of renovation, but.... Anyway, because of my family, as a child I could go to the operas. I loved them. And then a company from Venice came to do several operas. And they also did some improvisation—some "impro" they called it—with masks. Venetian Carnevale masks, wondrously beautiful gold and silver and black and brightly painted masks! The *impro* with the masks was magnificent; I can still remember! A man *or a woman* would put on the mask of a cat or a beautiful woman or a savage nobleman—*and become those things.* And do and say and become unimaginable things, unimagined even to the actors! I was a privileged child, I got to talk with the actors; they even let me hold the masks, and they explained them to me. They told me how the mask might *possess* an actor, and the actor does and says what the mask orders! How a mask might contain a good or evil spirit, might even be dangerous. They said the "mask" in Venetian really means the whole personality. The Venetian word is *masca*—and when a *masca* became the whole *persona*, and possessed a person, they called it **Masca**! Also they told me about, and showed me, what they called a neutral mask, or a "blank." It was not decorated or colored, it was white or colorless. And they said it was dangerous. But after all, how could a mask be dangerous? Absurd.

I must have been about fifteen, the age when a child thinks she knows something and must test the world

for herself. So I would test. While the Venetian company was here I got into the opera house in the middle
of the night—I don't even remember how. I do remember that I waited until long after midnight, so they
would not catch me! I went to the cabinet where the
masks were stored, and took some of them to the main
opera stage. The curtains were open. I managed to
turn on some of the lights on the stage. I began putting
on one mask, then another, and pretending to be what
the masks looked like. Before the empty opera house,
in the middle of the night, the little girl made her debut
in Grand Opera! As a Venetian noblewoman, a male
clown, a beggar, as many things. I had lots of fun! I
played! I was an actress. I acted, I pretended. One
mask scared me a little, I put it on—and I felt like a
two-year-old baby, I began to babble happily. But it
was scary, the mask began to possess me, I was not
myself. I jerked it off and was myself. OK! I know
what to do! If the mask scares me I just take it off.
Then I looked at the neutral mask. They said it could
be dangerous. I don't think so! I know better. So I put
it on.

*I disappeared. The mask possessed me, and I went away
and was replaced by someone I did not know. The Masca
completely controlled me, replaced me, and "I" could only
witness the work of the neutral mask.*

I was not afraid.

*There was nothing left of me to feel fear. "I" had gone
away, and all that was left of me was the Witness.*

*The opera house was full, it was jammed with people. My
debut, and I had a full house.*

They were not dangerous to me.

They all loved the Masca!

The Masca was a success!

The Masca—I will say "I"—*walked to the front of the stage. The front had been transformed, it was now a wide curve that projected out and over the audience, so that the people were now on three sides of me. I was close to them.*

I stood on the very front edge of the stage and looked out over a sea of people. I felt very safe, very beloved, and a series of vivid thoughts came to me. But they did not come as "thoughts," they came to me as facts:

I am one hundred years old.
I am dead.
But it doesn't matter, I am still here.
I am an ancient, dead woman.
I am the mother of all of the hundreds of people
        in this hall.
They are my children.
They are smiling at me, they love me. I am the
        mother of all these people.
I am God.
I am also a man, I am also a male God. They are
        both One.
I am God, female and male.
I HAVE GONE MAD.
I have gone mad.

I tore off the mask—or perhaps the Masca discarded me; it was done with me. I fell to the floor. I was there, screaming. Later I stopped screaming and I left. In the morning I ran away to Tinos, went to the Church of the Evangelistria, and told them I wanted to become a nun. I told them I was insane. In their wisdom, they took me in. I think, I know they must have contacted my family immediately and reassured them. I stayed at the Evangelistria for several years and was very happy. That is how I came to be known as 1003. That is all.

Oh, yes. And you want to know why I left the nunnery .... It was strange, you know. I became a nun because I had gone mad from the *Masca,* or thought I had. And I stayed happily as a nun at the Evangelistria for a number of years. In a strange way I must have been happy *because* I thought myself mad. This relieved me of all responsibility. I need only worship and serve God. This I loved to do, and could have done for all my life; to this day I wish they had allowed me to stay. They did not.

The nuns tried to tell me, very slowly, that the life of a nun was not my proper path. That I was not mad, that I was not a nun for the proper reasons, that I need not be there with them. But I was happy and would not hear. Finally the Mother Superior spoke to me with words that I could hear. She made sure I could hear. She shocked me into hearing.

Dear Mavros Angela, dear little Black Angel, you were never mad, we have told you this. You are the most beloved child of God. For reasons known only to Him, when you put on the Venetian Masca you became one with God. You know this now. But you are refusing to see what this means, so I must use words we don't ordinarily use: You are God. We are all children of God. We follow and serve and pray to Him. But where we hope and pray, you were, through the mystery of God, given. Where we work and hope and fail, you are given. You are one with God.

And that means you don't belong here, you are needed far more out in the rest of the world. You must contemplate what I have said, and pray to God, and then go where you are needed. Needed far more than here, where at least, God willing, we are on the proper path. Go back to the world and live simply, live simply as you are. This is all, this is all that you or any other need do. Go with God....

Yes. Go where you will often not even be appreciated. That is, after all, the way of Our Lord.

I don't believe this story. I think it never happened. But a voice says to me, "Write it in a book." I do not know what voice this, so I obey.

SIMENA: THE VILLAGE THAT WAS CURSED BY A WITCH

Simena, Kekova Bay, on the Mediterranean Coast of Turkey, is a small fishing village, the most beautiful I have ever seen. Half-submerged ancient buildings and tombs are strewn about the entire area, and the remains of a Genoese Crusader castle perch at the top of the hill. Lycean tombs and Roman and Byzantine Greek walls and gates, numb with age, mingle with the stone walls of Turkish homes.

Simena is paradise, a village of perhaps a hundred and fifty souls, ten families, on a steep rocky peninsula overlooking a protected bay of glass-clear sea. Simena has no road; unless one walks over the hills, it is reached only by the sea. The waterfront tile-roofed homes and restaurants each have their own small concrete quays. If you stood on the deck of a boat skimming the shoreline, you would see a dream-place of lovely cottages and homes on a hillside scattered with palms and ancient olives, and blazing with bougainvillaea. You would see a scattering of restaurant signs, a room or two for rent, many children at play in their little skiffs. Look closely, and along the shoreline sit massive foundation stones and the relics of sea-walls put there five hundred or a thousand years before Christ. Here is a Byzantine arch on a crumbling little stone shack, and near it a massive gate made of three huge stone slabs; on the gate is a Greek inscription—and on top of it, on the ruins, sit three satellite dishes.

Simena has no road, no cars, no policeman or doctor, no crime, no post office, no dogs—well, almost none. Simena has had electricity and phones since only about 1985. Everything comes from the sea, beginning perhaps 4,000 years ago with the Minoans and then the Phoenicians. Only the nomad Turks came over the land. Every morning the bread boat comes around nine o'clock from Üçağiz [do not try to pronounce words with this many wiggles.] The golden bread, long loaves stacked vertically in bright blue and red crates, stands like piles of yellow firewood against the flat deep blue sea. Then, several days a week, the vegetable boats come from Üçağiz. All day big boats and little skiffs bring tanks of water, which is laboriously piped or carried in large jugs up into the village. The jugs are sturdy plastic, but their plastic handles are identical in shape to those of 2,500-year-old earthenware amphorae. The shards of amphora now lie all about, buried beneath the packed soil of the village. The day-tour gulets, luxury motor-sailors, bring tourists and easy money from Kas or Kale, carry the tourists away by dusk. In the night there are no sounds but the distant rustle of laughter, the rooster, the little owls. The acetylene torches in the sky—are stars.

In Simena life is slow and seamless, of a piece. People say to me, "Why don't you live here?" Good God. I said to Nesrim, "I will if I can find a Turkish wife." She said, "I will try to find you one." Why would I think, even for a second, of staying in such a tiny place? Very simply, the people of this village have treated me with unimaginable friendliness. Most tourists come, race to the castle above the village, back to their boat, and in an hour or so they go away. So sad. I stayed twelve days, and people said—"Why don't you stay?" Why might I stay? Two clear reasons. First, I am an old man, and Simena is the only place I have ever known where, if I stayed and died there, a village would cry at my grave. And second, this is the only place where a beautiful girl ever fell in love with me without speaking a single word. I think sweet Sérife spoke only Turkish, but this will not stop a young girl in matters of the heart. On my first day here, a little hand took mine and led me through a mob of tourists, through a restaurant, out a low concrete quay, and tried to lead me onto a gullet. I explained to her—*we weren't invited.* She found both the concept, and my English, incomprehensible, but ever since that day Sérife has owned me. She sat often on my lap. Each time her Mother took her away, she came back. [She was only two-and-a-half-years-old.] And then one day I walked by the one-room home of her parents to find her in the path with a soft cloth rope around her waist, the other end anchored in a stone wall. The mother works; and in her explorations, Sérife is as mobile and fanatic as a raccoon. So—a leash. The tiny girl took one look—saw me—and, wordless, tottered over to my bare legs. She wrapped both arms tightly around my knees and buried her face against the skin of my thighs. And prepared to stand there forever. Her entire tiny being radiated the sad, incomprehensible, new and sometimes horrible discoveries of the tiny: first, not-invited-on-the-gullet— and now THEY-TIED-ME-UP, THEY-TIED-ME-UP, THEY... TIED... ME... UP... Sérife is an old and sober little soul.

In the morning a woman takes her boat to the island off the town, throws down chicken-feed and searches for eggs. The island is a coop. Her movements are slow and deliberate. When she steps back into the little skiff, she carefully lifts the offshore an-

chor, puts it in the boat, sits down, puts one hand in her lap. Then, with one oar in her other hand, gently turns the boat 180° on the water. Then she lifts her resting hand to the other oar, and goes home. Slow, seamless.

The men, boys and girls swim all day; boys simply live in the little skiffs and the water. Teenage girls, especially from Izmir and Istanbul, wear Western bathing suits. But one Simena girl has a proper mother, who remembers that only 11 years ago this village had no phone, electricity or television. Or uncovered limbs. One late afternoon this girl came down to the water, disappeared behind a skiff, reappeared swimming strongly far out ōn Kekova Bay. Little boys followed in skiffs; she laughed and smiled, clearly having a great time. However—strong swimmer as she was—she clearly wore a heavy long-sleeved shirt. And I think, she can't be swimming so strongly completely clothed! So I watched much later, when the girl returned from mid-bay and paddled deliberately behind the same fishboat. She bent, and seemed to labor briefly at some task. Then—having fully dressed—she marched out of the water in her soaked pantaloons and walked happily up into the village.

During the night an old man from the village died in the hospital in a nearby town. In the morning a boat brought the body back to Simena, but the family home was one room and the day was quite hot. Therefore the family divided the yard with drapes hung on a rope, and the old man was laid out on a table in half of the space. The men of the village, with many boys and babies watching, then cleaned the body, prepared it for burial, and wrapped it gently in a kilim. The Imam came from the mosque in Üçağiz, and the burial service was held. Much crying, wailing, celebration of

death and life, and the feasting went on for days. Only
a few hours passed before the ancient one was laid to
rest in the village burial ground. But during those hours
the old man lay in state with two ritual gifts on the table
beside his head: a vase of flowers, and a simple glass
of water. A member of the village was gone, a member
of the human family. He should not be thirsty on his
journey. Occasionally a villager would kneel beside the
body to see if the level had changed in the glass, to see
if he had taken a swallow or two. The Glass of Water,
ritual of a Mediterranean desert people.

Nur is a pretty seven-year-old, and Sadat is an angry
ten-year-old with the face of a medieval serf. Passing on
the narrow concrete quay, he buried his fist in her gut;
she curled up on the concrete and sobbed pitifully for
twenty minutes or more. Drenched in self-pity, the unhappy child may have been exaggerating her pain. Be
that as it may, shortly afterward the two mothers met on
a rocky shore of the village. Nur's mother is a foul-
mouthed brute, an unhappy, heavy woman whose life
has probably held little but labor and strife. And now
she was shrieking with rage at both the boy and his
mother, and the boy was viciously snarling back. With
half the village watching, what could Mother do but
defend her young? Raging, she gathered heavy stones
from the rock and pebble beach and raised up a heavy
stick. Her face and voice were indescribably savage. If
the stones flew... well, once not long ago in Simena a
woman with stones put a man into a boat to the hospital.
This time the stones did not fly—very probably because
Sadat's mother had come to the combat ground carrying
her tiny baby in her arms. Deliberately? God knows.
But, hit that baby with a rock? No chance. The village
would have killed the thrower.

The truth behind this seaside theater is rather sad. Apparently, Nur's is the dysfunctional family of Simena. It consists of Nur, her mother and father, and a grandmother. When the tourist day-boats arrive at the village, they are met by an urgent, clamorous little swarm of locals selling hand-decorated scarves. Most of these are young girls. But all three women of Nurs family sell scarves; it is the family business. The father sits home and sews decorations on scarves! The mother, an abusive and miserable soul, frequently screams at Nur and hurls objects such as half-empty water bottles at her. And the little girl, I am told, knows every last foul word in Turkish, and uses them. The women of the family are known in the village as Grandmother Witch, Mother Witch, and Baby Witch.

I have remarked that Simena treated me with great friendliness. In truth it is not difficult to make friends in such a small place, as one need only give of one's self. In Simena, where nearly all visitors are there merely for an hour or two, to visit for a week marks one out. It takes little more than a smile. All the little girls who sell scarves tried to sell to me—but in a few days they would pass me on a path, hold out their wares sadly and say *"Scarf?"*—and then, instantly smile broadly, saying *"No scarf!"* And chat with me in their few words of English. If I raised my camera toward one of them, she would scold me with her finger like an old grandmother. If I wagged my finger back, a broad smile followed. And then one late afternoon, as I sat in Barbaro's little restaurant with a coffee, the owner pulled up just below with a boat-load of wine. Barbaro and his family began unloading the heavy cases onto the quay; then they would be carried fifty feet up the steep rocky stairway into the café. My immediate impulse was to help with the labor, but I held back; as the only non-family worker, I would be conspicuous. Then two young Turkish soldiers who happened to be in the café went down to help. I instantly followed them and for ten minutes we all carried the surprisingly heavy cases of wine up into the café. (Barbaro's teenage daughter was carrying them effortlessly). I was dimly aware that a number of Turks were appraising me. I did the work innocently, but in fact it marked me out. So simple to convert from "tourist" to "friend." Barbaro never charged me tourist rates after the day his summer supply of wine arrived.

Regarding the scarf-sellers of Simena, one last remark is in order. Whenever day-visitors arrive, they are surrounded by a little cloud of children and a few older women selling scarves, and the tourists often feel badgered and harassed. Forty years ago Freya Stark described the villagers as very friendly but poor, able to offer a visitor only an egg and a drink of muddy water. Now Simena is prosperous from a modest summer tourist traffic, yet a present day observer of the tourist industry can write the following words: *The people of [Simena] are perhaps the greatest victims of tourism.... They no longer live in monotonous poverty, but their tiny patch of paradise is overrun....* Beware of educated people who sleep between clean white sheets but wish that others would be content to live in monotonous and illiterate poverty.

Every place and person has a White Legend and a Black Legend, and therefore it must be said: even Simena has a Black Legend, a dark side. [Shaw has eloquently pointed out the monumental boredom of a Heaven populated only by the docile and well-mannered.] The ancient ones of this village tell the story:

long, long ago the town cast out a witch [as I have re-marked, others still live here.] And as she departed, she cursed Simena with the most horrible words one could imagine in the Mediterranean world: YOU SHALL HAVE NO WATER. It brings to mind David's famous curse after the death of King Saul: "Ye moun-tains of Gilboa, let there be no dew, neither let there be rain, upon you, nor fields of offerings...." And ever since that day, Simena has had no water of its own — the water comes by boat. The people and gods of the Mediterranean are desert folks; they know how to value water, and how to phrase a curse. Parenthetically, that terrible curse means that the place has no water—but means that the paradise of Simena also has no mosqui-toes. I killed the last two.

The villagers cannot tell you how the curse was implemented, for it probably happened a thousand years ago. But I can guess. In Byzantine times, shortly after the curse and the casting out, a terrible earthquake struck the entire region. This witch applied indiscrimi-nate curses. The entire region, along the edge of the sea, subsided ten or twelve feet. Houses along the edge of the sea, including most of a Greek village across Kekova Bay, rather quickly found themselves looking up through ten feet of clear warm seawater. Some curse. What the witch meant, obviously, applied only to fresh water; all of Simena's ample fresh springs, which had surfaced near the edge of the sea, were now ten feet under salt water. But you may feel the effect of this curse! You, a thousand years later. Swim in the warm, crystal sea along the seafront of the village—and you will feel patches of cool water as you swim past the accursed springs of the outcast witch!

It is evening, and the Mediterranean light is turning gold on the beautiful wooden boats of Turkey. Butter gold. You are forewarned: if you come to this place, you may never leave. That is in the hands of Gods and witches—but also in your own. We shall therefore leave you with the words of Coleridge:

> *If a man could pass through Paradise in a dream, and have a flower presented to him as a pledge that his soul had really been there, and if he found that flower in his hand when he awoke —*

> *Aye, and what then?*

MY NAME IS ISAAC —
WHY DO YOU ASK?

Isaac was an orphan child of the slums of Istanbul, and he was six years old when he discovered the possibility of a life. Imagine, if you will, a ragged, dirty, wild-eyed, dark-skinned little animal despised by other children. Avoided by adults. Threatened by the clubs of policemen. The blunt truth, sad as it might be, is that Isaac was rather ugly and also quite insane. He heard voices.

His life was tragic, but the greatest tragedy for such a child was not that he was dressed in cast off rags. [His few new clothes never fit him very well, for they were stolen from clotheslines.] Nor was it that occasionally he was a bit hungry, for in the kindness of Muslim Turkey a child will almost always find charity food. Nor was his tragedy a lack of medical care; except for his frank insanity, he was as healthy as a boy can be. If such a child as this survives the first three years in the sewage-strewn wasteland of his home streets, from then on a bacterium would fry in his bloodstream. No, Isaac's tragedy was his treatment at the hands of other children. For Isaac was a freak. The others stoned him for recreation, cursed him on the alter of their own healthy superiority, urinated upon him for the relief of their boredom. I do not mean to exaggerate this child's misery; it would not be possible to do so. His waking life was that of a stoned dog, his sleeping hours were spent curled up behind debris in

the worst of alleyways. What chance for an insane orphan child who hears voices? Next to none. And yet....
And yet....

In a strange way, even for a psychotic orphan slum
child there is a certain strength in self-honesty. Isaac
knew he was crazy for most of his life. Knew that he
heard voices that others did not. He harbored no lasting hate for the children who abused him, for he knew
in his heart they were correct. *He heard voices. Nobody
else did.* Therefore, he was crazy, a freak. He did not
deny, to them or himself, that he heard voices. He went
right on with his conversations, his public dialogues
with these voices. To him they were real and not to be
denied. But at the same time, in a sane corner of his
brain, he accepted the primitive justice of his peers in
the slums: Isaac is crazy and to be stoned, *because he
hears voices.*

And then, when Isaac was six years old, a very
strange thing happened in his world: other people also
began hearing voices, voices that came mysteriously
from nowhere. And these other people were of the respectable upper classes. Allah! What to make of this!

Once, and then again and again, on the streets of
Istanbul Isaac saw a man or a woman who obviously
listened to voices, and replied, and listened again, to
voices—*and no one was there.* Others, beside himself,
respectable people with suits and ties, or beautiful
dresses and scarves, were also going crazy like Isaac!
But—obviously because these people were clean and
wore the beautiful clothes of the wealthy—no one
stoned them. Isaac could see, clearly, that all others
ignored the growing insanity of these well-to-do citizens. It was clearly acceptable to hear voices from the
invisible world of madness, even carry on dialogues in

public, if only one were well-dressed. If well and cleanly dressed, one would not be stoned. And Isaac began to study these people more closely. Perhaps something important could be learned. Even, perhaps, something that might lend him a hand up out of his world of stones and clubs and urine, and stinking alleyways. Just perhaps. *Enshallah.* God willing.

Little Isaac began to watch. Little Isaac had good eyes, even though his brain was a bit queer. And he began to see patterns in the behavior of these others who heard voices. Certain patterns. For one thing, only the well-dressed heard voices. For another, their madness seemed to be located in the left side of their brain, for often the person who heard voices would clutch—in distress?—the left side of his head. Especially in the area around the ear. And then on several occasions Isaac realized that the man—usually a man—was holding a small black box to his ear while he listened to the invisible voices. Perhaps it contained a medicine that made his head feel better or calmed the insane voices. Isaac wished he could find a black box like that; the voices in his own head sometimes said horrible things, and he would have liked very much to calm them. And then one day, praise be to Allah, Isaac obtained one of the small black boxes for himself and his life changed greatly. It happened like this....

On one warm October afternoon Isaac had left his home streets of western Istanbul and was roaming through the tourist districts of Sultanahmet, the old core of the city. The foreigners interested him; although they often seemed distressed, or afraid of the ragged little boy, they never abused him. As he walked along the park in front of Sultanahmet Mosque, Isaac saw ahead of him one of the new insane of the City—a well-dressed man talking to himself. Well, not exactly, he realized. As he drew closer Isaac saw that the man was standing on the grass lawn of the park facing a small tree. He was talking loudly to the tree or to himself, it was not clear which, and waving his right arm wildly at the tree. The tree, of course, was doing nothing at all, it was behaving itself. Certainly it did nothing to provoke this unhappy, shouting soul. And then, to Isaac's surprise and delight, this apparently respectable upper-class but crazed man completely lost his control. Allah! Who did he think he was talking to?! Suddenly he was shouting in anger, waving both arms at the tree—and he dropped the little black box he had held in his left fist. It fell to the thick grass lawn, bounced once—and Isaac pounced. He pounced, and never looked back, running furiously for the maze of alleyways a few blocks away below the Sultanahmet Mosque. No man and few boys in the City could have caught him. Isaac had his black box. He never knew, thinking back, whether the man had accidently lost his hold on the box or deliberately thrown it away. It was no concern of his. He had a box. A box of his own.

What little Isaac had captured from the grass lawn near the Sultanahmet was, of course, a cellular phone, a recent status symbol of the better classes of Istanbul. However, it would be years before Isaac discovered the objective realities of cellular phones; and in truth, for now he didn't need them. Not for communications. Safely back in his home alleyways the psychotic little child sat down, focused and businesslike, to review what he knew about the boxes and their users.

1) Their users, like himself, heard voices and replied to them—and no one was there.

2) Their behavior defined a mad person—ergo, they, like himself, were insane.
3) He had begun to suspect that these others heard voices in the boxes.

He put his black box to his ear—*and heard voices!* [How could he have known they were his own?] These facts to Isaac were monumental. In his mind, for the first time in his short life he had some small things in common with the others!

4) These others were clean and well-clothed, and *therefore,* he deduced, *therefore* were not shunned or stoned simply because they heard voices.

With these last facts—*the terrible importance of being clean and well clad*—Isaac saw hope for the future. And he set to work with fierce determination.

During the next few weeks Isaac studied carefully the details of the behavior of people with boxes. He entered, late on one black night, a very small window into a locked warehouse where certain valuable objects were kept. A few of those he traded to a man who sold good children's clothes. He knew an old man, once a friend of his long-dead mother, who worked in a hamam —a Turkish bath. From this man, trading on ancient ties, he obtained a bath and a haircut.

And then, still insane but clean and well-clad and with a haircut, the small child Isaac set out with his cellular phone to test the atmospherics of his great City. With his box held to his left ear, and his head tilted slightly to the left just like the others, Isaac sat on park benches and talked with his voices. He walked along the better boulevards. He stood on the green grass of the parks and talked to trees. Or to dogs, or garbage cans. But always with an attempt at dignity, and always with his box, like the others. And he listened to his voices, and discussed the matter with them. And the good people of the City DID NOT STONE HIM. They did not stone him.

What the good people saw, and thought, we cannot know. At a reasonable guess, they saw a middle-class child pretending to talk with what was probably a broken and discarded cell phone. They saw a child at play. But he was SANE. To them he was SANE. And to a degree somewhat beyond the hideous, we are—because we are social animals—we are what they think we are. They thought little Isaac was sane.

I have never acted in a theater in my life. If at gunpoint I were put on a stage and made to read MacBeth, the result would be ghastly—at best, something like low and very bad comedy. However, if you gave me five years to rehearse, and the flexible open mind of a child, I dare say I could manage a half-way decent MacBeth. And perhaps in this spirit—a spirit of rehearsal—the small slum child called Isaac set out to learn how to be truly sane.

How is one to be sane? Isaac had learned the first step: appear to be like the others. Now, at least for a child in his usual environs, Isaac seemed sane. He was clean and well-dressed and talked with the invisible spirits of madness only with his cell phone at his ear. He managed to maintain this facade for a few weeks, and to his satisfaction the other children of the slums no longer stoned him. If to you this is a surprise, consider what would happen if someone—you yourself, perhaps —were blessed with a visit from the Almighty. Wonderful! Wonder-full. However, one should not now go about in public saying joyfully, "*We are all One!*" They will put you away. The lesson: *keep the hard truths to yourself.* Isaac kept his hard truths to himself.

Next Isaac addressed the difficult problem of his private, insane voices. Public appearance was under his control, well and good. But Isaac was truly an intelligent child, and he saw clearly that his private voices were unusual. Did they brand him irrevocably as mad? No, Isaac reasoned, of course not. His were rather more cruel than most, but he saw—decided, needed to decide, for the sake of his own stability—that everyone heard voices. You, yourself at this very moment, for instance; you are hearing voices that say "*This is an entertaining story!*" Or, perhaps, "*This is not a believable tale.*" No, Isaac decided his voices were to be made manageable, and gradually the voices became more quiet. More sane.

The next problem was the objective reality of the cell phones. Isaac had taken his first steps away from madness through a happy misperception of the use of the boxes. However, intelligent as he was, he soon saw that the usual sort of cell phone was a device through which the good people of Istanbul talked with each other. One might imagine that this would destroy his carefully invented new reality. Nothing of the sort. Spunk is genetic, and Isaac was of tough material. He simply expanded his world. With his cell phone as cover, and a joyful exploratory drive as his gift, he set out to master the cellular phones of Istanbul. He learned the proper use of his own. When its owner was billed for its use, and cut it off, he stole another. And another. Finally he found a gifted electronics man—a Turkish mafia functionary, perhaps—who somehow wired a phone so that it worked without billings for quite a long time. His private voices came to him less and less frequently. Their malevolence slowly subsided. And with his cell phone, little Isaac, the mad orphan slum child, set out to make a living.

Isaac was six at the beginning of our tale. Soon he was seven, then eight, nine. With better and abundant food, his body thrived and his small intense mind grew large and shrewd, but his face always remained strangely incongruous in relation to his body. It was, oddly, the face of a world-weary middle-aged drifter, for Isaac never really was a child and he had never known love. What he did know was this: in Istanbul little boys beg on the street; but men of little talent or education made their living hustling customers for the fifty thousand stores of the City. Especially the carpet stores—carpets and rugs were where the money was. The process was simple: a man, a hustler, determinedly strikes up a conversation with a tourist. These thousands of hustlers are the bane of tourist Istanbul, swarming and relentless and hysterically ignorant of truth in advertising. If such a street hustler levers a tourist into a carpet store and that person buys a carpet, the hustler gets 10%. Or 20%, or even more. The amount is negotiable. Isaac set out to be rich, and Isaac had his own methods.

Wandering the streets of Sultanahmet with its thousands of tourists and thousands of shops, Isaac made himself a calculated, deliberate curiosity. What in the world is this strange child-man with a cell phone on his left ear?

"No," he would say with dignity, "I am certainly not a beggar, and I don't want to sell you anything. Why should I? But if you want, as a favor I will tell you there is only one honest carpet store in Sultanahmet. It belongs to my family. If you want to look, it is _____. If you tell them Isaac sent you, they will treat you especially well." The fortunate store sold several carpets to Isaac's tourists in the first month for a gross of about $5,000. Then the unknown "Isaac" sent a strange little boy with a cell phone to pick up his commission. When the store gave a percentage less than requested, it suffered shortly afterwards the unfortunate fracture of its largest sheet of plate glass. The immediately adjacent store suddenly experienced a serious burst of prosperity. It thrived. So did Isaac. He was a master hustler and he was on his way. In a few years the little slum rat was moderately rich. Only moderately sane, but definitely prosperous.

Then, searching for meaning in his life, as we all do, Isaac made his first serious mistake. He began to think seriously... about his sanity. And introspection—ach, it is full of hazard. Who can look in a mirror and see himself?

I first met Isaac when he was thirty-seven and in the last year of his life. He was now, for all practical purposes, a sane man; he was moderately wealthy, and now was known by his proper Turkish name: Ishak. What you have read of his childhood is exactly as he told it to me. I say this only because of the harsh terms he used in reference to Isaac the child—I myself would never, for instance, have called him an animal or a slum rat. Ishak told me that he had made a serious mistake in examining his own sanity. In fact, the mistake was a whopper; he had decided to see a psychiatrist. One can perhaps find sanity through either magic or Western psychiatry, but one cannot—*cannot*—have both. [Any more than one can nudge two large chunks of plutonium together and ask that they simply sit there.] Ishak described to me his meetings with the psychiatrist. They went something like this, after the preliminary history was taken.

"Doctor, am I sane? And don't lie to me. I raised myself on the streets of this City, and with that training I will see any lie."

"Ishak, what do you mean by sane?"

"Doctor, that is unworthy of you; it is both an evasion and inherently a lie. *Am I sane?*"

"Ishak, you are essentially sane. Don't you agree?"

"Thank you, doctor."

"As sane as most people, Ishak."

"Doctor, you give with one hand and take back with the other."

"Ishak, does what I think matter? Isn't your own opinion the one that matters?"

"Not correct, doctor. We are what they think we are. By the way, are you aware that you often answer a question with a question?"

"Ishak, does it matter?"

"Forget it, doctor. There is something else. Apparently I am fairly sane, but I am not a whole human being. Men are comfortable with me, some of them, and think I am normal. But women sniff the air near me and then run away. They say I have no love in me, nothing. Apparently this is important. Doctor, I know there is something missing. What can a man do if he has raised himself as a slum orphan and never known love?"

"Ishak, what do you mean by...? No, I should not ask this question. Ishak, I don't think I can help you with this. But if you will read Nikos Kazantzakis' story of his visit to Mount Athos, it is possible you will understand what I am about to say: *God is in women.* I cannot help you any more. I wish you luck. Goodbye."

"Thank you, doctor. I think I was correct to choose a woman psychiatrist. Goodbye. Oh, one last thing. Doctor, are you married?"

"Ishak, why do you ask?"

Ishak left the psychiatrist's office after his last visit with the doctor, and went to his home. He went to the locked desk drawer where for 30 years he had kept as a momento, perhaps as a Holy relic, the cell phone he had snatched from the grass near the Sultanahmet Mosque. His first black box. In his mind the long-dead cell phone was the device that had delivered him to sanity. And he knew now this was simply a device. But like all truly sane people, and even the half-sane, Ishak also believed at times in magic. This was such a time.

Ishak put the dead cell phone to his left ear and said, half in seriousness and half in humorous despair, "Box, talk to me."

"Who is this?" said the box.

"This is Ishak! Who are you?"

"I am Isaac. The little slum rat. And I am the black box who changed you into Ishak, into what you are to-day. The black box you discarded in a desk for thirty years, after I showed you the way from the slum or-phan to Ishak. And I am something more, someone more. *Repeat after me, to me:"* [The box began to speak in Turkish.]

"Box, I do most of my business in English. That passage was originally in Hebrew. It would be more familiar to me in English.... Say in English."

The Lord is my shepherd; I shall not want
He maketh me to lie down in green pastures:
He leadeth me beside the still waters.
He restoreth my soul: He leadeth me in
The paths of righteousness for his name's sake.
Yea, though I walk through the valley of the
Shadow of death, I will fear no evil: for
Thou art with me; thy rod and thy staff
They comfort me.
Thou preparest a table before me in the
Presence of mine enemies: thou anointest
My head with oil; my cup runneth over.
Surely goodness and mercy shall follow me
All the days of my life: and I will dwell
In the house of the Lord for ever.

—Psalms 23:1-6

"Box, who are you? *Who are you?*"

"Ishak, I told you; I am Isaac. I am a cell phone. I am also Allah. God. Ishak, does it matter? If it does, *why* does it matter?"

"WHO ARE YOU?"

"I told you, Ishak: A box. Isaac. Allah. Why? Why does it matter, why are you sitting here at your desk talking to a cell phone, dead these thirty-one years?"

Then the box began repeating the 23rd Psalm in the reversed first person, as God. The box thought it was God....

"I HAVE NO LOVE," screamed Ishak.

"So," said the box. "You have discovered the last, final truth; Life without love is not worth a bent penny, or the body of a dog ten days rotted.

"YOU HAVE MADE ME SANE BUT NOT WHOLE."

"What has that to do with me? Love is not a commodity, like sanity. One can fake sanity. Not love. Love cannot long be manipulated. It has naught to do with black boxes, but rather with the final saddest fact known to mankind: *One is loved if one is loveable.*"

Ishak slowly put the black box—or Isaac, or Allah, or whatever it had been—back in the drawer. He slowly locked the drawer—and as an afterthought, dropped the key in the wastepaper basket. Going to the kitchen of his flat, he poured a glass of raki; slowly, thoughtfully, he drank it and poured another. And another. With each glass of raki he became more calm, more clear about his destiny, more happy with the bottle of raki. More courageous.

It might have been one or two in the morning when Ishak returned to his desk, retrieved the key, opened the drawer, and again took up his original black box. It said nothing. He placed it in a coat pocket and walked for ten minutes or so to the Golden Horn and the Galata Bridge. Now, one can see through the waters of the Golden Horn in bright sunlight for about five inches. In the late 20th Century it is the most terrible of sewers. At night it looked as dense and cold as asphalt.

Ishak climbed up on the east railing of the Galata Bridge with his box. He brought little Isaac, the orphan slum rat, with him. And he brought Allah with him— no, of course I am mistaken, Allah was there waiting for Ishak. Allah is everywhere and beneficent. Allah is love.

Ishak sat with his friends—with little Isaac, his box and with Allah—on the east rail of the Galata Bridge. He held the long-dead cell phone to his left ear. And he asked,

"O God, my God, why hath thou forsaken me?"

A soft voice replied, "Ishak, Ishak, why do you ask?" It was a clear evasion.

Ishak released his hold on the Galata Bridge and watched in only mild surprise and curiosity as the cold black asphalt of the Golden Horn raced toward his naked eyes.

KISS ME AGAIN IN VENICE

Rosina was the youngest of the three or four maids that usually worked at my little family hotel in the Connaregio, the old working-class district of Venice. All of them were smiling and friendly with me, for I usually stayed for two or three weeks in this lovely city where most visitors manage one or two days. The other maids were usually heavier, middle aged and sometimes a bit tired; but Rosina was perhaps twenty-four, and full of humor, full of sparkling energy. In her maid's uniform, hard at work on the rooms, the floors or toilets, of course she could not be at her best—but at eight in the morning she always had a light in her eyes and a smiling *"buon giorno."* Rosina was always proper; she was married, she was a good Cattolico, I am sure. But then, on the day and the very hour that I was to fly away, Rosina wanted me to kiss her goodbye. What could I possibly have done....? This is the story of Rosina and her kiss, and of her humor and her gifts and her beauty. And it is also a story about cowardice.

The first couple of times I stayed at the hotel, Rosina was memorable only for her warm cheerfulness. Often I would be at breakfast when she arrived for work, and always she had a bright smile on her face, another *"Buon Giorno."* She had a good job, worked hard, and stayed firmly in her role of hotel maid. Dear reader, you must understand that in Italy roles are important! Italy is a country where roles are central and stereotypes are the ordinary reality. Its grand music is Grand Opera. Its love songs are Neapolitan, its savagery is Sicilian, its avarice is Venetian. And every Italian is playing roles in this theater; most of them are convinced that given the opportunity they could sing *at least* one role in *La Forza Del Destino*. Most Italians feel that the world is their own individual La Scala, even if in fact they live in La Casa Del Mutilato! And sweet Rosina played very well the role of hotel maid. Then I saw her in another....

In the Mediterranean, even in elegant, patrician upper-class Venice, there are egalitarian moments. Moments when all men and women are equal before each other and before God. This was a very special evening. Luigi, the hotel manager and son of the Patron, the owner of the hotel, was marrying his childhood sweetheart! There was a splendid wedding party, a feast at the family restaurant. That wonderful restaurant serves the most authentic Venetian food and the most superb wines to be found in all Venice. The Patron is the chef. The entire family, including Luigi and his bride, were playing host and waitress—and among the fifty or sixty guests, dressed in their Sunday best for a magnificent sit-down dinner, were all the hotel help. *Including all the good souls who swab floors and clean toilets.* Rosina was there—sleek and charming, beautifully dressed and polished. In an hour or so she had assumed a new role; and I should be ashamed to admit it, but I was surprised that the maid who cleans rooms could in hours turn into this Venetian Lovely. The next morning, or perhaps it was two days later, she was again at the hotel at eight o'clock in her white uniform.

You must realize, dear reader, how consciously and easily the Italian changes roles. I shall give an example. A few years ago I was sitting with friends on a terrace half way up the cliff overlooking the loveliest fishing port on Procida, a little island a few miles off Naples.

Capri floated in the distance. Vesuvius, the sullen metaphor for all sleeping menace, sat on the southern horizon casting smoke into the sky. And here below us on the calm water of the harbor came a little fishing boat full of people. The owner stood and thrust forward on the oars, over and over. His half dozen passengers, probably paying tourists, sat quietly while the man labored on the two heavy oars. My friends, my hosts, knew him and called down from the cliff, waving and holding up their glasses of *vino rosso*. The visitors' guide looked up, saw his friends—and instantly changed roles! *Now he was a Simple Neapolitan Fisherman!* He burst into a roar of Neapolitan love songs, worked more joyfully at the oars, and cast a wide, sardonic grin at the watchers. And on the cliff dozens of Italians burst into appreciative and equally sardonic applause.

Months before the time of Rosina's kiss, I had left Venice and traveled east to Istanbul. And at breakfast before my departure, in front of the three other maids, she had said with loud and sorrowful tones, "Sandy, you are going away today? Where are you going?"

And I had replied, "Greece, Turkey, and perhaps Syria."

Instantly she jumped into a crouch, flung her arms wide in mock despair, and loudly shouted, *"Take me with you!"*

Quickly I stood a bit more straight. I examined her carefully and thoughtfully for a moment, and then said in a very deliberate voice, *"Rosina, be very careful what you ask for. It may be given to you."*

In the smallest fraction of a second, she bent her body into a defensive cringe. Throwing her right arm toward her face as a shield, she pathetically held out her left hand toward me and cried, almost whined, "*I have a husband!*" On that left hand her gold wedding band glittered cheerfully.

"*I am so sorry, Rosina,*" said I, "*but we can't take him with us.*"

And while everyone in sight collapsed with laughter, poor frightened Rosina once again cried, even more loudly, "*I have a husband, I have a wedding ring.*" She held out the gold ring as if to ward off the devil himself; and as I think back, it would have been a nice ending flourish if she had crossed herself in mock terror. Perhaps she was not a good Cattolico girl, after all....

Three months later I was back from the East for a few days in Venice. Then I would fly home. Again, on my arrival everyone at the hotel greeted me with the warmth of old friends. So lovely to be treated like that... But a week later I was repacking my bag for the flight from DiVinci Airport to Amsterdam and San Francisco. Since the maids had taken good and friendly care of me, for many days in all, I would leave each of them a small present. However, for Rosina, after the hilarious "*Take Me With You!*" episode, the present should be more special. In Istanbul for a trivial price one can buy a lovely silk scarf; perhaps sixteen inches by four feet of soft pale lavender, and stamped in gold with a Sultan's seal in Arabic calligraphy. In Venice it would be costly; in Istanbul, a very small matter. I gift-wrapped the patch of lavender and gold, went down in the morning for my last breakfast—and dear Rosina was not there. It was her day off. Oh, well. I would have enjoyed seeing her face. But I left it with the kind woman at the desk, asked her to pass on the gift, and dismissed it from my mind. More important, I must now inventory my money, passport, tickets, the notebooks and treasures from months of travel, and pack. Two hours later I was packed. I must leave in minutes for the airport—I was doing a last check of my little hotel room —and a knock came on the door. A soft knock. I opened the door. There stood Rosina in street clothes.

"The desk, they called me and told me you left me a present. I came to see what it was." A long pause. "*It is so beautiful,*" she said softly. "*Why did you give me a gift like this?*" Rosina was speaking very quietly in a small voice, but with deliberateness. With a firm but puzzled tone, she was trying to attach meaning to the bit of silk. Her own meaning. I explained that it was a simple token of affection; it had not cost me a fortune.

"I don't know to believe you. Nobody gave me a gift like this.... It is so beautiful. *Thank* you." She paused again. She seemed to want to say more. She could see my packed bag. I must leave for the airport. We said a last goodbye. Finally—and here at the end of it was a beginning—in the fashion of the Mediterraneans we kissed each other goodbye on the one cheek, and then on the other cheek. A pause. Then she said quietly,

"*Kiss me again.*"

I will hear that voice all my life. She had never spoken like that before. It was not polite, it was not patrician, it was not comic or seductive or gentle. It was, very quietly, an instruction.

"*Kiss me again.*"

I stared at her face. Her chin was tilted up toward mine, her mouth was slightly parted. Her eyes were fixed on mine, we were locked, suspended, standing still in time; her voice was the businesslike, bored instruction a slightly dominant Italian wife might use on a husband of thirty years:

"Kiss me again."

Our mouths locked. Quickly, devouring, hungry, unimaginably sweet, sweeter than the sweetest wine ... I was acting quickly, before my wretched brain could kick into gear. Drowning. I was drowning, so was Rosina. She began to thrash in my arms, then we were on the bed.

"Your husband?" I asked.

"There is no husband."

"My plane," I said.

"There is no plane. That is your ticket on the dresser? . . . There! There is no ticket." The fragments fell to the floor, fluttering down. She stepped on the bits and glared with satisfaction.

"There is no ticket!" she repeated. "Kiss me again."

Lost, I was lost, it was like falling from the high deck of a ship into the sea. On the bed. Thrashing, first one of us and then the other above, below, clawing. She bit me!

"Take off my bra —Do I have to tell you? How long? —Use your mouth! USE it, you fool! — NO. Not here, THERE!"

Then she was screaming, with a corner of the pillow in her mouth. Then she was sobbing.

Rosina lay beside me for a few minutes, exhausted. She was a miracle. Then she stirred. Her eyes opened, deep wells of satisfaction—no, I was wrong.

"Kiss me again. I am not done." [Then she began reading my mind!] "No, you are not going. We are not even begun." [The ticket, you silly woman. It cost money!]

"No, you have not lost the stupid plane. I will tell

the manager at DeVinci that I, the maid, lost your ticket. He will give you another. You don't want it now! Kiss me again. —Now, I am almost finished, roll me over, yes, now, yes come in yes now. —OH! Oh, Oh, Oh God...." Then she was screaming, screaming, clawing at the pillow under her face. It exploded and the room was filled with feathers. We were covered with our own juices; the feathers came down all over us, and Rosina was babbling, half unconscious. Babbling, confused, she turned her head and looked up at me and saw—

"The feathers! Forget the feathers, fool, I am the maid, I will clean your room.—Not your room? —Of course it is your room! —You gave it up?—NO! I looked at the book, you are still booked in.—Was it in Luigi's handwriting? No, I don't think so— oh. I gave myself away, didn't I?"

"Well, kiss me again."

"The woman at the desk? She - yes, she laughed, of course. What she thinks? Why should you care? Well, she is not any trouble. She is my aunt."

"No, you do not get up now. Go to sleep with me now.—What are you doing sitting up and looking at me like that?"

"THE TRUTH?"

"WHAT IS THE TRUTH...."

"WHAT DO YOU MEAN, I CAN'T COME IN YOUR ROOM?"

"WHY?"

"NO. NO! Don't tell them, please."

"No-o-o-o-o-oh...."

So that you will understand what I truly did at that moment, I must offer you my last recollection of Rosina.

It may not be completely realistic, for my thoughts have
been twisted by sadness into something a bit doubt-
ful....

She is standing quite tall and still now, 5'8"—at the
door of my room. Her large hank of black hair is tied
in a bundle down the side of one shoulder. Her eyes,
her face, her thick eyebrows, are all dark with calm
speculation. Her chin is up, her eyes are slits. Her short-
sleeved blouse is white, thin, edged with lace against a
skin of absolute, untouchable bronze. The blouse is low
cut in an elegant swoop against that bronze, and it is
edged with white lace. Around her neck, against the
bronze and white, lie a fat gold chain and a longer string
of gold-colored beads. I think she wore a bra, but it
was thin. Her breasts stood up like heartache beneath
it, and her nipples were round and dark. Rosina was
an apparition out of Verdi. A dream. She waited.
Waited. She opened her lips one last time and said,

"*Kiss me again.*" Forgive me, I may not remember
correctly, I *think* she said,

"*Kiss me again, you fool*" [*let me come in your room*].

I kissed her once again ... on both cheeks. She said
goodbye. I went to the airport with my ticket intact,
and I flew away.

THE STONE DOLL

He picks up in his hands things that don't match --
a stone, a broken roof-tile, two burned matches,
the rusty nail from the wall opposite, the leaf that
came in through the window, the drops dropping from
the watered flower pots, that bit of straw that the
wind blew in your hair yesterday -- he takes them and
builds, in his back yard, approximately a tree.
Poetry is in this 'approximately'...
    —Yannis Ritsos

The following story is fiction. That is, bits and fragments that I have built into, approximately, a story. It is true that some of these fragments have to do with actual people; we are all of us broken pottery, our shards are scattered everywhere on the surface of the earth. I have simply picked over these bits and pieces. If one of these fragments is larger than the others—if indeed this story has a prime flesh and blood subject— then I will name that person in winter when the last leaves are falling from the tree.

A crescent hangs in the evening sky. The water is very calm; no wind. A hazy bank of clouds stands low in the west over Keros. On the ferry quay several little children play about. The sun falls under the western clouds and suddenly the belly of the sky is bathed in myriad shades of pink, rose and flame. The sky ignites. In a silent thermonuclear rage, softly it consumes itself. All Katapola stands silent, perhaps a little awestruck, facing west. The children, immobile, stare at the sky, three little girls side-by-side holding hands. And then the unthinkable; under a crescent moon and backlit by the dying flames of the sky, they join hands to make a circle and begin to dance. Wildly they dance.

In my acute loneliness I register the internal state of all around me. I imagine that soon their clothes will disappear, their personae vanish. Their skins will peel, and all that will be left is muscle, bone and quivering nervous system. This last will thrash about and generally insist that life is quite satisfactory. That it is having fun.

Several Kalymnos fishing boats are in port sheltering from the gales. In quiet periods they fish. The old fisherman brought swordfish to the taverna and had it cooked for us. It is his pleasure, but also a poker game of gift-giving. Another younger man enters the game and raises the stakes: buys Santorini white wine, mussaka and salad for all. The Kalymnos fisherman is stern as he surveys the table. He leaves, comes back in a few minutes with a large lobster to be cooked for the gathering. "I raise one lobster—and four beers." The lobster does not know it is in a poker game. It crawls feebly across the checkered table waving its broken legs and antennae, and it thinks, "I am not having fun. I can't believe these people are going to boil me." But they did.

Children are playing a schoolyard soccer game. The smallest of them are very fast and good with their feet. Many of them hold their shoulders high. Smile, laugh, shout. This world is for me, they sing. But one older girl, perhaps thirteen or fourteen, is different. Not the splendid black mane of hair, hers is limp and straw-brown. She is a bit heavy. Round shoulders hide the breasts she cannot understand, and her arms and fists are iron with rage. She is screaming, shrieking with rage. For many minutes. The boys are cheating her. The ball is hers out of bounds, and they simply take it. Twice she grabs a boy heavier than she, slams him to the ground. The boy does not retaliate; perhaps he is forbidden to manhandle a girl this age. But she is done for. Vomiting pain and rage, she gestures obscenely over and over again. Desperately she fights the dying of her light. Once. "MALAKA" lances across the schoolyard. She is done for. Homely. Branded as difficult. Obscene. "I am not having fun," she thinks. "I am not. Now I will never have a husband on this island. **Difficult.** I can't believe they're going to cast me out." But they did.

> *You see how it is*
> *in the kingdom of the naked,*
> *in the kingdom of*
> *open people; sometimes the open door*
> *closes. On a traveler.*
> *A fish. A little girl. And what*
> *can the poor fish do—*
> *in a world full of laughter*
> *and music, hot sun, and*
> *Dimitra's horn filling the harbor*
> *and the little owls singing*
> *all thru the night.*
> *All thru the night.*

Once Upon a Time, in a land very far away from any place else, a little girl was born to a poor family. Her mother cleaned rooms; and God the Merciful took her father when she was very young. As a small child she was not unusual; she was just like the rest of us. I do not remember her as extraordinary. She was not very beautiful, but in a Mediterranean world this is not important. What matters here is that the girl is good, and will make a proper hardworking wife. When the little girl was perhaps six years old, however, her life became extraordinary. While playing in a field near her home she found, and took home, a beautiful and ancient little white stone doll. I have never seen this doll, although it still exists and its location is known. It is said that the doll is glistening white; perhaps it is of the superb Cararra marble, or Palestinian alabaster, or even the sacred white stone of Paros.

The little girl took her doll home, washed the soil from it, and was told by the village teacher that it was very old and valuable. This last word she did not fully appreciate, for what is "valuable" to a child? She would be enlightened in good time, but for now she sewed dresses for her doll. In her hand it developed the patina, the soft aura, that always comes when a thing is loved. And then an old Greek, traveling far from Athens, came to her home port—and heard of her beautiful white doll, came, looked, and offered money for the doll. He clearly could not have known the people of this country, or much of children, for he was asking a sacrilege; he was asking a mother to sell her child. For lesser offense than this, the gods have done hideous things to men.

The Greek returned to his distance home, unsuccessful in the usual game of buy-low/sell-high. Would that this was the end of it, but a month or so later he returned to try the game of barter. "I have brought for you, from my faraway world, a **Real** doll. It is pink, like real dolls, much larger than your little stone doll, and she has many beautiful dresses. Dresses made in famous Athens, of which you have heard! And I will trade this doll for your poor stone doll (I will trade this Real, city-made doll for your only child!)." Since this is a fairy story, and we all know the rules of fairy stories, I need not tell you the answer to that. However, the Greek remained on the island. He did not leave.

You must know a small detail about life in this remote place. Imagine you are here now, sitting in a café on the waterfront over a mid-morning coffee. The Mediterranean light, glittering bright and warm, pours down on the deep blue harbor, and music pours from the café. The houses are white, the fishboats come and go with their trims of bright color, the vegetable truck stops by the water and the man hangs his scales over the tailgate. The gypsy peddlers are tying a load of woven baskets on their own little truck, tiny children underfoot. You might, except for the details, be in Genoa or Kas, Andros or Jerba. But one particular detail you might not be able to see. Here, in the old days, nobody locked a door. Still, in the last days of the millennium, many do not lock their doors. Some doors do not even have a lock. And then—the stone doll was gone. The little girl's child, perhaps the only child she would ever have—disappeared.

The little girl gradually grew into a larger girl; a young woman; a mature one. And in doing so, she made a series of discoveries. Some were painful. Who knows about stone dolls? "Archaeologists." She became an archaeologist. What is necessary to have a husband and children? "One must be docile and subdued." Oh. This she could not and would not be. And therefore...a loss. When she began University studies in archaeology, she found that in places where German and English are spoken, the museums are full of marble and gold and jewels stolen from her country. Worst of all, in the University she discovered that she herself, a little girl from a poor family in a remote provincial village, was far more intelligent than practically anybody. That can be very lonely. And, last of all, she found her doll. In a place where French is spoken, in a museum in one of the great cities of Europe, because she was an archaeologist she found her childhood doll. Now she could trust no one.

Who? Who, who could she trust? God? God had taken her father. The boys of her village? They wanted her not. They called her difficult. DIFFICULT!! Trust The Greeks? A Greek stole her doll. The English, the Germans? They were robbers. Trust her teachers at the University? She was far more intelligent; she saw all their limitations, heard all the echoes of their false confidence. The French? Trust the French! They were fences, buyers of stolen goods. Child-buyers! She hated them! The Arabs? The Armenians? *The Turks?* Come on. The Jews, the ...? In the end—in the end she was left with only one person to trust, herself, and this.... this is the hardest thing in the world. This she could not do. Unable to trust anyone, she became afraid, and fear is a crippling thing....

As an older woman, the little girl came to love deeply and passionately the one thing she had loved as a child: the stone doll, archaeology. The two essentials of a human life are love and work. [Papa Freud said that.] Nothing else is comparable. The stone doll became her love, her work—in fact her obsession. Archaeology became the universe. There is little similarity between a small love and a small obsession. However, between a great love and a great obsession, there is no difference at all. The little girl became one of the great archaeologists of her country, known and respected over much of the world. She developed immense intelligence, and became an immensely energetic and powerful woman. A woman of great ability and at times of considerable charm. And beneath this: distrust and fear. Her few superiors she impressed. Her peers she treated with care, as is proper. Her social and professional lessors, however, and those she employed, did not fare so well. They were to be used, and used mercilessly. And regarded with contempt. Every city and every person has a Black Legend. This archaeologist, merciless in pursuit of her stone doll, had a Black Legend: she was respected by all, and loved by none, a terrible thing to say of anyone if it were true. It was not true. But within archaeology, yes, it was true. Outside of her obsession, she was kind—and that is a different story.

Her domain, her protected territory, became the Mediterranean coasts which had produced her. She came home. Came home and became the fearful, and protective and fierce guardian of the soil that had thrown up her stone doll. Woe be to the villager who wanted to dig a well, the visitor who wanted to put a little house on a nearby island. Allah protect the farmer plowing a new field or the tourist bending over to pick up and examine an ancient shard. Or, for that matter the man who kneels at an archaeological site to tie his shoelace! One might as well want to dig a subway in Athens or Jerusalem! *Or build an airport on her home island!* Suddenly, standing in the yard or flapping across a plowed field like some great and vengeful crow — here would come an apparition screaming "NO. NO.

NO, STOP!" And she had certain power behind her, the power to make difficulties. She *was* difficult. Enough. The end of it—

This archaeologist and myself have large and over-lapping obsessions, both Mediterranean. After great effort I was able to obtain two brief interviews with her. I wanted her opinion on one legitimate and simple archaeological question. She could have answered. There is a legitimate answer. I needed an answer. In the first meeting she avoided the question. In the second, she lied. Then she ignored an agreement.

This is the story not of one woman, but of all who find it difficult to trust. Perhaps many of us have been mugged. After one is mugged a few times by fate, trust is damaged. Only the heroic can rise above that. Lord knows, I cannot. I am annoyed that the archaeologist will not trust me, that she answers me not—but after all, why should she trust a stranger? She was mugged yesterday in Kolonaki. We were, all of us, mugged yesterday. Who among us looks at a purse-snatcher and sees God? Not I. Not I. I cannot.

I will confess that in the beginning this sketch was based on a very real Mediterranean personality, a quite important and difficult woman. At first her face, her huge intelligence, and her unkind qualities hung before my mind's eye as I wrote. But increasingly, as I wrote on, what came before my mind was my own damages, my own limits, my distrust, my rage. Distrust of *her*? Dislike of *her*? Contempt from *her*? "Of" and "from" are merely prepositions. I started out to write a story— a story in which I would tell of people as they are. I fear that I have been sitting at my writing table, scribbling— and looking into a mirror. The subject was not the stone doll; the doll simply had a high polish.

I set myself the task of writing of people as they are. A man sets himself the task....

> *A man sets himself the task of drawing the world. As the years pass, he fills the empty space with images of provinces and kingdoms, mountains, bays, ships, islands, fish, houses, instruments, stars, horses, and people. Just before he dies, he discovers that the patient labyrinth of lines traces the image of his own face.*
>
> —Jorge Luis Borg

THE BOY WHO PLAYED CHESS WITH DEATH

Chess is simply a game of war on a board. It is important for this story to understand that those knights and castles are exactly that. Those pawns—are meant to be slaughtered. The bishops? Over much of the history of Western Civilization, bishops have made or blessed or bankrolled war, or caused it to be made. And at the end of the game of chess, at the moment of *checkmate*, death lies waiting. The goal of chess is to kill a king.

When the Germans finally conquered Greece during World War II, after heroic Greek resistance, they turned the occupation of most of the islands over to the Italians. However, the Germans needed the magnificent natural harbor of Milos as a staging area for the invasion of Crete; they took Milos for themselves, and built major naval facilities. During the first year of the occupation of Milos, the Germans took food from the Greeks, and Greeks starved. [In fairness it must be said that when German supplies were adequate they *gave* to the Greeks.] There were executions of Greek hostages; Greeks died in work battalions, and as the by-product of Allied bombing. On Milos, the war was a time of savagery....

One day in 1943, two fifteen-year-old boys sat on a stone wall in the Plaka of Milos, the main town, playing a game of chess. The town is at the top of a nearly sheer cliff, and looks out over one of the most magnificent harbors in the Mediterranean. One of these two boys was named John Ninos. While the chess game played out in the warm sunshine, two passers-by stopped to watch. One of these men was the commander of the German occupation forces that ruled Milos. On this man's orders, many Greeks had died. On this man's whim, any living thing on Milos would die. The Kommandant was Death himself. And Death stopped casually by the side of the road to watch two Greek boys play a game of war. The game played out. John Ninos won. The Kommandant moved to pass on, then paused and said a few words to his aide. And that worthy, who spoke a little Greek, said to John Ninos terrible words: *"You are to come to German Headquarters Building at four tomorrow afternoon--to play a game of chess with the Kommandant."* [Come and play a game of chess with Death.]

Ninos went the next day at the designated hour and played that game of chess with the German Kommandant of Milos, and neither you nor I can truly imagine what that was like. Ninos was a boy of fifteen. You cannot imagine a child could be in jeopardy playing a game of chess? This is a question of imagination, and on wartime Milos men, women and children had died for unimaginable reasons.

Ninos found the Kommandant a very good player who made errors not consistent with his abilities. The game went slowly, the German eventually left a castle in a position where it should not have been left. And in the end, John Ninos killed a king. Did the Kommandant let a Greek boy win? So one might speculate. However, when the German saw checkmate approaching, a brief but real flash of anger crossed over his face. Perhaps, as we know happens in war, the man had simply underestimated his enemy. After all, the enemy was a child....

The Kommandant said to Ninos, "So. You have won. What do you want for your reward?"

And pride spoke firmly, "Nothing."

But an aide was ordered to make a package of candy, sugar, toothpaste, coffee, mostly those things a boy would like and which had not been seen on Milos for a long time. Such, perhaps, is the act of a decent man who does hideous things—toward a boy who plays war with Death and kills a king.

Toward the end of World War II, the German Kommandant of Milos and two aides were ambushed and killed on the island by Greek and British commandos operating from Kimolos. One of these companions was a German doctor who had given medical care of high quality to many Greeks on the island.

John Ninos now lives in upstate New York, the father of many children and grandchildren. He says that long-ago incident allowed him to believe that there was something human in those people. John Ninos is a man who played chess with Death. And won.

A PROPER WAY TO DIE

Adrianou is a small street in the Plaka of Athens. Few cars are allowed—it is mostly a walking place. And here, early on a warm and quiet evening in October, a very old and bent woman shuffled slowly along. Bent.... *Broken* is a better word. She was small, and her back was bowed so that her face was exactly toward the ground. Her old, long, faded, dark blue dress hung flaccidly down. Her lower legs were scaled and ancient posts. Her shoes appeared to be floppy, old, oversized men's gym shoes, without laces but fastened shut so that they now were slippers. The socks were dark circles collapsed around her ankles. The woman's face was that of an ancient and shopworn peasant, with rounded and lumpy features. She wore the omnipresent piece of cloth around her head. An old and poor peasant woman, easily seventy or eighty, she probably had buried all of her own and now waited for death. He would not come as an enemy. Every Greek village has one or two such, living out their allotted time apparently steeped in fatalism.

The two of us passed on the gradual slope of Adrianou as she plodded by, headed up-slope. After we passed, something made me turn and glance over my shoulder. What it was I did not know. But I glanced, then faced about, stood there in bewilderment, and finally followed her back up Adrianou. I did that. I was in something like shock, for reasons only gradually conscious. The old woman shuffled very slowly, moving one foot ahead. Then she would stand for a full second, pause, and then move the other foot. Occasionally she paused for five or ten seconds, immobile. A plastic bag hung from each of her hands, a cane was under one arm. Her face, as she walked, was always directly toward the ground. Once, when Adrianou was briefly empty before her, she navigated a diagonal course across the street toward a building. Perhaps she could see little, but at one moment a girl-child raced across Adrianou in successful pursuit of a kitten, and the old being turned and followed this out of the corner of her face for many seconds. A little later she found her way blocked by a tourist staring into a brilliantly lit window full of gold jewelry. Obedient to the prevailing reality, she also faced the window full of golden light and stood immobile for many seconds. What thoughts dwelt on the gold chains—or on anything else? Then she turned, and one old foot moved deliberately up Adrianou's blazing canyon of light. Stopped, paused—and the other foot obediently moved. Finally, after one of these long pauses, I realized why I was gripped by the old soul. She would pause periodically on the gradual slope, pause for many seconds, almost as if trying to decide whether to bother going on. She looked as if walking into death.

"I might not bother," she seemed to say. "I just might not bother. Enough is enough. **I don't have to take another step. I could just stand here—and die**—and then just stand here until somebody bumps me. And then I will fall over."

I stared at her with something like mild horror. That was what made me turn about. And follow. The old woman looked—I can sum it up—she looked as if the motor might stop. At any second. The motor was prepared to stop. At any step, during any pause. Now. Or now. Or surely at this time tomorrow. This body was peacefully prepared to stop, to die and to sleep. In the middle of the street, God willing.

I want to learn to love and hate like an Irishman; and learn to love women so that my blood does not trail where I have walked. I want to hug many children. I want to love light like a Sicilian, and accept death like a Greek. By the time I am 94, like Berenson, I want to identify so completely with the not-self that there is no self left to die. And then, at the end I want to die like this old woman. I don't want to die in bed. I won't. I want to stand here in the middle of the street and peacefully let the motor stop. I just won't bother any more. Then I will just stand there. Until somebody bumps me.

Then I will fall over.

ABOUT THE AUTHOR

Sandy McCulloch is a Corvallis, Oregon, writer and photographer who spends several months each year in the Mediterranean. He has been a zoologist, college lecturer, psychologist and an innkeeper. Sandy has also been involved with mental health services in both California and Oregon. He has three children and two granddaughters.

Other writings by Sandy McCulloch describe the Greek Cycladic Islands, and he is presently working on a new book on Mediterranean ports. Asked about his beliefs, the author says:

"The Mediterranean culture is very different from our own, in many ways more kind and generous. Mediterranean commercial ethics are more relaxed than ours. Arguably, their Gods are closer and their children more dear to them. Perhaps, then, these stories contain the sub-text of forgiveness. Perhaps we need to forgive one another for being so different, one from another—for in the important matters, we are all so alike."